BULL ★ RIDER

BULL RIDER

SUZANNE MORGAN WILLIAMS

Margaret K. McElderry Books
New York London Toronto Sydney

MARGARET K. McELDERRY BOOKS
An imprint of Simon & Schuster Children's Publishing Division
1230 Avenue of the Americas, New York, New York 10020
MARGARET K. McELDERRY BOOKS is a trademark of Simon & Schuster, Inc.
For information about special discounts for bulk purchases, please contact
Simon & Schuster Special Sales at 1-866-506-1949 or business@simonandschuster.com.
The Simon & Schuster Speakers Bureau can bring authors to your live event. For more
information or to book an event, contact the Simon & Schuster Speakers Bureau
at 1-866-248-3049 or visit our website at www.simonspeakers.com.
Also available in a Margaret K. McElderry Books hardcover edition
Book design by Krista Vossen
The text for this book is set in Alinea.
Manufactured in the United States of America
First Margaret K. McElderry Books paperback edition May 2010
8 10 9 7
The Library of Congress has cataloged the hardcover edition as follows:
Williams, Suzanne, 1949–
Bull rider / Suzanne Williams.
p. cm.
Summary: When his older brother, a bull-riding champion, returns from
Iraq partially paralyzed, fourteen-year-old Cam puts away his skateboard to enter
a $15,000 bull-riding challenge to earn money to help his depressed and
rehabilitating brother pull his life back together.
ISBN 978-1-4169-6130-7 (hc)
[1. Bull riding—Fiction. 2. Brothers—Fiction.] I. Title.
PZ7.W66824 Bu 2009
[Fic]—dc22
2007052518
ISBN 978-1-4424-1252-1 (pbk)
ISBN 978-1-4391-5668-1 (eBook)
1011 MTN

*To my husband, Reed, for his constant and
sustaining support, and to the troops who served
in Iraq and Afghanistan and their families.*

ONE

Folks in Salt Lick say I couldn't shake bull riding if I tried. It's in my blood, my family. Around here, any guy named Cam O'Mara should be a bull rider. But if you've ever looked a sixteen-hundred-pound bucking bull named Ugly in the eye and thought about holding on to his back with a stiff rawhide handle, some pine tar, and a prayer, well, you'd know why I favored skateboarding. My grandpa Roy, my dad, my brother, Ben, they could all go as crazy as they liked, sticking eight seconds on a bull for the adrenaline rush and maybe a silver buckle. But me, I'd take my falls on the asphalt. I'd master something that I could roll under my bed when I was done with it. Or so I thought.

It was June and my big brother, Ben, was home on leave from the Marines. He started in on me about the skateboarding. "Cam, I'm gonna break that thing and then you'll have time for something really extreme." Ben's five years older than me, which is enough difference to mean he didn't beat on me the way some older brothers do, but he wouldn't leave me alone, either. "When are you gonna stop being some wannabe skater punk and do rodeo?"

"About when your head pops off and rolls down the street like a soccer ball." I jumped toward him like I was going to knock his head across our room with my knee. He faked right and punched me in the stomach. I smashed into him with my shoulder, and we both fell on the floor to wrestle. It took Ben about four seconds to pin me and press my face into the rug. I spit wool hairs out of my mouth.

"Give? Give? Skater wimp?"

I never give, and he knew it, so he held me down until he was tired of it, and then he slapped me on the back and let go.

"You coming in early with me to the rodeo?" he asked.

"Sure," I said, getting up and trying not to favor the shoulder he'd had a lock on. It was weird to have Ben home again. I'm not saying it was bad, it was good. It's just his hair was buzzed from being in the Marines, and without his cowboy hat, he seemed stiff and different. Maybe the year overseas had changed him. But when he pulled the hat on, well, there he was, my brother, Ben, again.

See, Ben's a cowboy and so am I, I guess. I mean, I help out on the ranch with the cows. But Ben's a *cowboy*. That's his thing. He was Nevada State High School Bull Riding Champion and all. And I really was glad he was home. The timing couldn't have been better. School was out, and the rodeo at the Humboldt County Fair was on. Grandpa Roy'd put in the money for an entry—it was enough for a new skateboard for me, but that wasn't in his plan. "I know Ben doesn't have much time at home, but what else would he want to do but get in the bull ring? He's an O'Mara, and we'll give him the best we can while he's here."

So, Ben was bull riding again—like he'd never been to Iraq at all. Even my six-year-old sister, Lali, knew that was big. She'd been bouncing around all day, asking when we were going. It was almost time, and now that Ben was done squashing me, he rummaged in his drawer for his lucky socks. He'd worn them the first time he won at bull riding, and now he wore them every time there was a prize on the line.

"You don't need those socks, you know," I said.

"You're sounding like Mom. And what makes you the expert? Did something change when you turned fourteen?"

"You can ride any bull, just like Grandpa. I'm just saying you don't need luck."

"I can always use some luck." He grinned at me.

Now that was funny. I'd never known anyone as lucky as Ben. He got the good looks and the bull-riding gene—there has to be one in this family—and, geez, he was already grown-up. That counted for something. Me, come August, I had to face Mr. Killworth, "the knucklecruncher," in ninth grade. That's my luck.

Ben found his socks and pulled them on. They looked regular enough—gray work socks—but he'd worn the fuzz down to a shine on the bottoms. That's what happens when you wear lucky socks enough times. Next came the boots. Those took some serious tugging. Then he reached for his belt with the champion buckle.

"Remember when you won that?" I asked.

"Well, yeah."

"I carried your bull rope."

"And I wore my lucky socks," he gloated.

I threw a cushion at him.

"Watch the hat," he said.

At the fair, Ben's luck just kept flowing. Even the weather was good. The thunderstorms that had been predicted held off, and the stands were full. Dad bought pop and ice cream for us, and Lali about jumped out of her skin, waving at the girls in their satin shirts and bright new jeans who galloped in carrying the flags. I was wired up, counting the minutes till the bull riders and Ben's go-round.

His first bull was young and wanted to run around the ring instead of bucking. But he got a reride. The second time he drew Son of Ugly. Now, *that's* a bull to score you some points. 'Course he wasn't as mean and nasty as his sire— they say no one's ever rode Ugly. But the offspring gave Ben a wicked ride, hopping and twisting and kicking up a dust storm. Ben made his eight-second time and sailed off.

The high school girls covered their eyes and shrieked when Ben landed. The guys slapped him on the back, and he disappeared behind the chutes, king of the bull ring. It was almost enough to tempt me onto a bull, but not quite. Ben was the champ. He was the one Dad and Grandpa bragged on to their friends, not me. He could have it. I wasn't him, and I wasn't going to try to be.

I pushed my hair out of my eyes and spotted Mike Gianni, my skateboarding buddy, and Favi Ruiz in the stands. I jumped a rail to get over to them.

"Man, Ben is great. You don't ever want to go up on a bull and do that, do you?" Mike asked.

"Naw."

"Cam's smarter than that," Favi said.

"Bull riding's not about being smart; it's about being gutsy," I said.

"That's my point." She looked at me like she'd won something. Favi's father was foreman on our ranch, and they lived next door to us in the Old House, where my Grandpa Roy was born. I'd known her all my life—like a sister, almost.

"You don't need bull riding. You're better on a skateboard anyway," Mike said.

"Best around," I said with a grin.

"Except for me. How much longer is Ben in town?"

I blew some air out of my mouth and shook my head. "A couple more days."

"Man that's harsh," he said.

"Yeah, it is," I agreed. At my house no one talked about when Ben was going back to Iraq. But now I'd said it. Two more days.

On the way home, I rode with Ben. The windows were down and the air blew around us, warm and sweet smelling from the sagebrush.

"You ought to start riding," he said.

"It's not my thing."

"Well, it should be. You could be one terrific bull rider."

"Naw," I said. "Not like you and Grandpa. You almost

won and you haven't been on a bull in a year. Second isn't bad."

"It's the socks."

I laughed and pinched my nose. "Yeah, it's that lucky smell."

"Man, those socks smell lucky *and* sweet," he said, and we laughed until I snorted. When we settled down, the night seemed extra quiet. The tires hummed on the pavement, and after a while a pack of coyotes got to yipping as we drove by.

"So, why do you have to go back?" The question stretched out between us. O'Maras don't talk about uncomfortable stuff. The coyotes wound themselves into a frenzy—howling and yelping till my skin bumped up.

Ben ran his hands up and down on the steering wheel. "They extended everybody. You know that. I've got three more months."

"It's not fair."

"Lil' bro', I might sign up for another year in Iraq after this. I'm thinking about it."

"Why?" I stared at him. "I thought you were coming home. You're gonna win big money on the pro circuit and take it and raise bucking bulls. That's what you've always said." Ben had run on a hundred or so times about his plan to me and Dad and Grandpa. O'Mara Bucking Bulls—that was his dream. So, I hadn't one clue as to why he'd want to forget all about it, about us, and be gone for more time over there.

"There's guys that need me. They're short on replacements."

"Somebody else can do it. You're a bull rider."

He looked at me like I was just a little slow. "I'm a Marine, and like I said, guys need me."

"Well, make them give you some extra armor or a desk job or something."

"Don't need it. My guys got my back." He put a stick of clove gum in his mouth and held the pack toward me. "So what'd you think of that Son of Ugly?"

"He looked like a Sunday picnic kind of a bull to me."

Ben reached over to grab me, but this time I ducked. The truck swerved and Ben swung it back and forth a couple times across the empty road, and we laughed till it hurt.

Two days later, Mom and Dad drove Ben in to Reno and he flew back to Iraq. Mom started marking the ninety days off on the kitchen calendar. Dad ran the video of Ben's high school championship ride again. There was Ben hanging on out of the chute, hand up, bull spinning. You can't exactly see his face on account of the hat, but I knew what it looked like. It looked just like it did when he whooped me at wrestling or when he beat me racing our horses and looked backwards over his shoulder and grinned a long, long time. I knew that look by heart, so I slipped outside with my dog, Red, and my skateboard.

✷ CHAPTER ✷

TWO

Before I tell you more, you probably want to know why'd he go anyway? Didn't he have it made, being Nevada State High School Bull Riding Champ and moving up to the pro circuit? Why'd a good-looking cowboy like my brother go be a jarhead? Well, if you lived in Salt Lick, you'd know. You almost have to *look* for Salt Lick. It has two churches, a bar, a Grange Hall, a feed store, and a gasoline/grocery that sells Mexican food on the side. It has a new post office and a boarded-up antique store that Mike's mom, Ella Gianni, opened and closed in the same year.

In Salt Lick, we know everybody, and half the town is related to each other somehow or other. Every family has somebody who came back from Vietnam with a Purple Heart or somebody who didn't come back at all. The grandpas, they march in the Veteran's Day Parade, and you can still get a good story about World War II on Friday night at the Grange Hall if you go early enough to catch the old geezers.

Sure, some folks think different, one way or another about politics, but everyone has one thought about the United States. If it's in trouble, we go.

And that's what Ben did. He passed up college and the pro bull-riding circuit, which everybody said he had in the bag, and joined up with the Marines. Everyone thought that was just fine. Except my mom. She held her tongue, but you could see in her eyes it broke her heart. Paco Ruiz signed up too, and Corey Henson. That's half the senior-class boys, off to the service. We gave 'em a barbecue out at the salt lick.

Salt Lick really has a salt lick, and it's smack in the middle of our O'Mara Ranch. It's a big white hill of salt. The cows love it. And it's a good thing it's on our ranch because the cattle come from all over, and then Dad and Grandpa Roy and me get the ATVs and run them back where they came from. But the O'Mara cattle, they just stay put and lick to their hearts' content. Grandpa Roy says that salt makes 'em grow strong and fat. He figures it's something like magic, O'Mara salt. I figure it's salt.

Summer time, the salt lick is the best place for a party. The salt sparkles in the sun and where the salt stops, the sage and rabbit brush struggle to grow along its edges. A little ways farther is a big swath of low pasture. It's green out there and there's a creek and cottonwood trees off to the side. Grandpa Roy says, "It's God's very paradise." Cow or human, don't matter, the salt lick is perfect. So after Ben graduated from high school and signed his four-year contract with the Marines, we sent those guys off with barbecued steaks and enough pie and watermelon to sink a ship.

And, of course, while we were there, some of the old guys got to telling stories about how that salt was famous, all the way back to my great-great-grandfather, Sean O'Mara's times. They told all sorts of stories about it—how if you put it in your whiskey, it would cure a bald head, or if you threw it over your shoulder when the moon was up, your girl couldn't resist you. Each one tried to tell a bigger whopper. It was like the Salt Lick pastime.

And stories or not, time passed. That's the summer I learned how long six weeks can be when a guy's in boot camp, with Mom perched by the phone waiting for Ben's calls. She'd answer on the first ring when they came, talk fast, and then say, "He says it's hot and he doesn't have time to be homesick. He sends his love."

"Did he say anything else? Anything?" Grandpa would ask.

"No, his time was up. But he sends his love."

See, in boot camp, you don't get to call the outside world but every so often, and when Ben called, he only had two or three minutes. Mom would pretty much put to memory what he said, then call his friends and tell 'em over and over. It made her happy.

After those calls, I missed Ben—a lot. So I'd take my skateboard and go to Mike's house. When you're feeling down, skateboarding is the best. It's all about speed and control. And if we weren't boarding, we watched Mike's DVDs of Tony Hawk showing ways to do nollies or checked out podcasts of new skate tricks on the computer. Some high school guys at McDermitt had set up an Internet server, so all the ranches were online. At least if Ben had to go away, I still had Mike around.

— ✳ —

When he was done with boot camp, they sent Ben to more training. He passed, of course. Ben came home on his first leave looking taller and stronger. That's when I learned that a guy does what he's dealt in the service. "It's Iraq," Ben said quietly. "Well, that's what I signed up for, right?" And once he was over there, I thought about him less. A year is a long time.

I got to do more stuff around the ranch with him gone. Some of that was cool, like handling the branding iron at the spring calving, and some of it was plain hard work, like digging out willow starts to make more room in Mom's garden. And sometimes, at night—if there'd been a report on TV about another Nevada soldier who was killed in Iraq, or if they'd shown a twisted up marketplace that exploded in Baghdad—I heard Mom whispering to Dad in their room and crying.

So having Ben back home on leave in June was great. It was like we were real brothers again. Seeing him bull ride was more awesome. I didn't believe he'd sign on for more time over there in the war. I believed everything would go back to being the same once he got done with the three-month extension and missions outside of Baghdad and came home to Nevada, or even California—that was close enough. But I was wrong.

It was the end of August when we found out about Ben. Mom had just marked off a day on the calendar. She had twelve more squares to cross off before he was done in Iraq. That was about the same number of days Lali and I had been back in school. It wasn't long at all.

That morning, I walked with Lali and Favi to the end of the ranch road to wait for the school bus. The cottonwood leaves scraped against each other. A handful on the biggest tree had turned gold. That was a sure sign that fall was coming—even more than starting back to school. Soon enough, the bus stopped and we climbed on. I found my seat next to Mike. The driver folded the stop sign into the side of the bus with a bang, and we rocked onto the dirt road.

"Dad put a calf down last night," I said to Mike. "It was real sad."

"Why'd he put it down?" Mike asked, taking the bait.

"Well, its mom ate too much salt out at the salt lick. It was born with two heads, and it was trying to walk in both directions at once." I said it just as calm as pie.

Mike's eyes went wide. "Two heads, really? Did you take a picture?"

I burst out laughing and punched Mike on the shoulder. "Got you again, yeah, I did."

Mike punched me back. "I knew. I did. There's no two-headed calf, not in Salt Lick, anyway. You're just full of gas."

I grabbed Mike's arm and shook him till the bus driver slowed up and glared at us in the rearview mirror. So I pushed him away and stared out the window. I didn't see any two-headed cows, but there were regular cows. Plenty of them. They didn't look up, didn't even twitch.

Sun beat down on the mountains. Sagebrush bent in a

stiff wind. The road turned, and Salt Lick peeked through the cottonwood trees—Salt Lick, population 675, except on school days, when the bus brought sixty extra kids to town. It was a lousy day to be going to school when I could be training my colt or riding my skateboard. Instead there was Killworth to face and a whole day of sitting in class in front of me.

When we piled off the bus, Lali waited for me by the flagpole. "Tie my shoes, Cammy."

"You're big enough to tie your own shoes. Remember how Grandpa Roy showed you about the loops being like bunny ears?"

"I want bunny ears," Lali said. I knelt down to tie up her sneakers.

"Let's pretend we're bunnies now." She started hopping around.

"Hold still, Lali. I can't do this while you're jumping." I finished and tied a double knot. "Okay, go, or you'll be late to first grade." She waved as she walked backwards toward her class.

I ran to my own class, in the junior and senior high building, and managed my one macho move—showing up at Mr. Killworth's room just as the bell rang. I slammed down into the chair just in time. But Mike and Favi were late.

"What exactly is it that's more important than getting to class on time?" Killworth asked.

"I dropped my backpack and everything fell out. I'm sorry," Favi said.

"Was Mr. Gianni in your backpack too? Is that why he was late?"

"He was helping me pick up my stuff," Favi said.

"And he can help you clean desks at lunchtime. Now take out your social studies books, all of you." He wrote "August 27th" on the board.

With Killworth we were lucky we all didn't have to clean the whole school. He nodded to me. "Cam, read out loud starting on page thirty-seven."

I flipped through the pages till I found the place. *The Great Depression was a hard time for families. Drought ruined farms, banks closed, and workers lost jobs. Some families had to start all over while others clung to their traditions to get by. . . .*

Just then, an office helper poked his head in the door and held a note toward Mr. Killworth. "What's that?" Killworth grumbled. He read the note and said, "Cam, you are needed in the principal's office." His voice turned oddly gentle. I stared at him.

"Take your things, you won't be back today."

Everyone looked at me. Something was really wrong.

✦ C H A P T E R ✦

THREE

Grandpa Roy stood by the counter in the principal's office holding Lali by the hand. His face was gray.

"What's wrong?" I asked.

"We're on our way, then," Grandpa said to no one in particular. He straightened his cowboy hat and led Lali out. I followed.

We got in the truck. Grandpa opened the half door to the little seat behind the cab and belted Lali in. I hopped in next to Grandpa, and since he never talks until he's good and ready, I waited.

But Lali didn't. "Grandpa, Cammy says you can tie my shoes like rabbit ears."

"He does, does he?"

"Yes, and can I get a rabbit? I want a black-and-white one, please."

"Lali, not now," I said.

"It's okay," Grandpa said. "You can have one if it cleans up after itself."

"Oh, I know it would—if you told it to, Grandpa."

Grandpa burst out laughing. "Lali, you are special."

But then he stopped talking altogether, and Lali leaned back and hummed to herself. It was the longest drive, waiting to find out what he wasn't telling us. It was long but it was fast. Grandpa was on a tear. We turned away from the ranch, past the Giannis' house and the Baptist church. Grandpa hardly slowed down for town.

Finally, he spoke. "Your mom and dad took off for Reno about a half hour ago, going to the airport. It's Ben. . . ."

"What about Ben?" It took me a second to sort out. "Is he okay?" I asked. "He's okay, isn't he?"

"Not hardly. No." He chewed on his bottom lip and glanced at Lali, who was still singing. He lowered his voice. "They went and shot him." Grandpa fixed his eyes straight ahead.

Shot. The word echoed in my head. Shot. Shot. They couldn't shoot my brother, even if he was in the Marines and in a war. He was too tough for that, and too good, and he was my brother. "Don't tease me," I said. "What really happened?"

"I can't hear you," Lali said from the backseat.

"It's nothing, pumpkin," Grandpa said.

"But I want to hear."

I got what Grandpa was trying to do. "It's just boring stuff," I said. I looked over at Grandpa Roy.

"Really, he's been shot," Grandpa whispered now. "They flew him to Germany early this morning, and they'll bring him home to the States, probably to Bethesda Naval

Hospital, in a couple of days. Your folks are on their way east to meet him. Your mom wouldn't wait for the military to send them tickets or anything. She says she'll be there when Ben comes in, period. They should be settled in DC tomorrow, and they'll call when they see him."

And there it was—the thing that changed everything.

"Where are Mommy and Daddy going? Will they take me?" Lali asked.

"No, pumpkin, you're staying here with me."

"But where are they *going*? Are they sleeping over? They might get lonely."

"Don't worry. They'll just be gone a little while," Grandpa said.

I knew Grandpa wanted to be on that plane back east with Mom and Dad, but instead he'd come and got us for company. Ben was his favorite. Ben and Grandpa Roy, they shared something tight and special—maybe it was the bull riding. They were both champs. Or the height, they could pass for brothers from behind. I take after my mom—stocky and dark, but tall like the O'Mara men. I was almost as tall as Ben already, and Ben's just past six feet. But he's blue-eyed and sandy-haired, just like Grandpa. And there's no changing either of them once they make up their minds.

The rest of the morning was a blur. Grandpa yanked the wheel and whipped the truck into the lot at the Feed and Ranch Supply store. "How a man can run out of fence staples, I can't figure," he told the clerk.

"I think you used the last one," Lali said seriously.

"That's telling him," the clerk said. He handed her a peppermint.

All that racing was for fence staples. "At least we didn't have to go the hour away to Winnemucca," Grandpa said. "Had what we need right here in Salt Lick."

Grandpa drove back through town and turned up the ranch road. Gravel pinged against the truck and a tail of dust rose up behind us. We stopped by the north fence. It figured. When Grandpa needs to chew his thoughts around in his head, he does something useful with his hands—he mends fences or digs out stumps or hammers on a roof. That's what he did that day. Grandpa and I wrestled barbed wire all morning. Lali handed us the staples until she got bored and went off to pick wild sunflowers.

Now, barbed wire can jab you, but I wouldn't have felt it. My brother was lying bloody and broken somewhere between Iraq and here. The whole time he'd been in Iraq I'd tried to tune out the news. I didn't want to know the stuff that could happen. Favi sent letters to the soldiers over there and kept track of the bombings and such. But not me. I turned off the TV or changed the station on the radio when they brought it up. It was easier not to know.

But now my mind went crazy. I wondered where he got shot and how. Did the blood splatter all over? If the wound was nasty enough, did your brain keep it from hurting? Did he scream? "No," I said out loud. I shook my head to stop my thoughts and fixed on the barbed wire. I unrolled it slowly so it didn't go snaking around on its own. Grandpa wrenched it tight against the fence posts. He braced himself, leaning into the wire tool, while I hammered in the staples. We did it over and over. I tried to forget about Ben and everything but the fence wire and the wind. Lali whinnied and galloped like a horse until she ran herself out, curled up in the truck, and fell asleep.

When we got back to the house, the whole scene got bigger and stranger, the way it does when everyone you know gets involved in something. Mom and Dad called from Denver while they waited for another plane to Washington, DC. They talked to Grandpa but not to me or Lali. That was weird. Mom always made sure she talked to everybody, even if Dad complained about the phone bill.

Then Amy Jones called. She's our neighbor, and when she's not thinking about cosmic energy and people's astrological charts, she pulls her hair into a ponytail and does ranch work like everybody else. She and her husband, Neil, have the biggest place around. They run a lot of cattle, but it's Amy's side of the business that brings in the money. She sells little frozen vials called straws that ranchers use for AI—artificial insemination. They use the stuff to get their cows pregnant from prize bulls without having to haul the animals across the country. Sometimes Amy called Grandpa about business. But today, I figured Amy wasn't calling about cattle breeding.

"Amy's got a prayer meeting going at the church tonight," Grandpa said when he hung up the phone. "It's a potluck."

"Are they praying for Ben?" I asked.

"We all are."

Lali, she just kept going, the way a six-year-old does. "Oh, let's take green Jell-O. *Please*, can we?" she asked.

"Green Jell-O it is," Grandpa answered. "Clean up your boots and change those jeans," he said to me. "Your mother wouldn't have you going out like that. And comb down your hair." I took my time.

Grandpa Roy drove slowly to the Baptist hall. The parking lot was full, and the lights were on. I balanced the Jell-O, pushing backwards through the double doors and into the long hall, past the Ladies' and Men's rooms, past a framed cowboy prayer and a picture of the Paradise High School Roping Team. Past the junior high mural of "Broncs in Heaven." There was a photo of Pastor Fellows leading cowboy church before a rodeo and six portraits of Salt Lick's rodeo queens starting in 1943. And there was Grandpa Roy, young and spunky and grinning, his champion belt buckle catching the camera flash and shining with a starburst at his waist. Only his blue eyes were brighter.

Grandpa Roy was a legend. There wasn't a bull he couldn't ride, not even the one that hooked him and stomped his hip. I knew the story by heart since I was little—how Grandpa lowered himself onto the bull in the chute. How the bull was so still in that bucking chute it gave Grandpa the shivers. How that Brahma burst out like he exploded when the gate opened—a nightmare twisting underneath Grandpa. It threw up both back legs at once, then turned to the right, then threw his head back till Grandpa could see the white around his eyes. But Grandpa held the rope around that bull's middle, balancing himself, almost floating above its whirling muscles. He finished his eight seconds and beat that bull and flew off. I'd heard the story a hundred times. Grandpa'd say, "The bullfighters threw their hats and slapped the bull to draw him away. On any good day, I'd have been up the fence in a minute, but that crazy Brahma's eye was right on me." Well, he hooked Grandpa Roy with a horn and then stomped solid down on his hip. Grandpa scored ninety-two out of a hundred—forty-six each for him and the bull—and plenty high to take the win, but it was the end of his riding. He could stand the pain for sure, but the hip wouldn't heal enough to hold on. Grandpa rode his last bull twenty years before I was born.

Now Grandpa tested his cell phone reception as we walked down the hall. The connections were crazy around here—seemed like it depended on the wind or sunspots, maybe. I just wished it would ring. I wanted to hear Ben was all right.

The tables in the church hall sagged with food. Someone had taken Ben's picture off the wall and propped it between the trays of peanut-butter brownies and lemon bars. Ben, arm held high, held on to a twisting spotted bull.

"I'm hungry," Lali said. I filled a plate for her, but I couldn't eat.

Favi sat with her mom and dad, with her back toward me. Mike nodded at me, but he didn't come over. Everybody got quiet when they saw us. "It's not like he's dead," I said to Grandpa. "He'll be okay."

"Sure he will," Grandpa said. "'Specially if these folks can do anything about it."

The ladies served their paper plates and moved toward the folding chairs. Darrell Wallace came over. He'd only just turned twenty, but right then his face was so serious that he looked old. I didn't know what to say to him. He and Ben were always trying to outdo each other in the bull ring. But Darrell went hot and cold with Ben depending on who was winning. Once, when he beat Ben in a big competition, Darrell had the name of the bull he rode tattooed right on his wrist. He turned to Grandpa. "Let me know if there's anything I, well, any of the guys, can do."

Grandpa put his hand on Darrell's back, and they stood that way for a minute.

"It could have been me," Darrell said. "If I'd enlisted, it could have been me. I can't believe this happened to Ben."

Pastor Fellows cleared his throat. "Let's take a moment to bless this food."

Then Grandpa's cell phone rang. He answered. A baby whimpered and his mother shushed him. The whole place was quiet. Grandpa kept saying, "Uh-huh."

When he hung up, the Baptist hall seemed to let out a breath.

"They say it's his skull," Grandpa said softly. "There's a problem with his brain. He's in surgery."

I couldn't pull enough air down into my lungs. I wished time would go backwards—back before Ben went away, back before they shot him, back the way it was yesterday.

"His brain? Is he paralyzed?" Amy Jones asked.

"Don't know yet," Grandpa whispered.

"What's par—a—lized?" Lali asked. "Is it a pair of limes?"

"They want to know if he can walk," I said.

"'Course Ben can walk," Lali declared.

"He's in a coma," Grandpa said. "They won't bring him out of it until his brain heals some."

Everyone broke out talking at once. I couldn't see Grandpa Roy for all the people gathered around to shake his hand and wish him well. I got my share of hugs myself, and Lali ended up on Amy Jones's lap. As things settled down, Pastor Fellows didn't bless the food. He skipped right to a prayer for Ben. I didn't follow it. I made my own prayer—the kind of thing you don't share out loud.

FOUR

There we were, just a piece more than a year after the send-off barbecue at the salt lick, and we were praying in the Baptist hall while Ben lay halfway around the world with his brain smashed up. Ben had some shrapnel in him, but we didn't know much else about what'd happened. Except they called it TBI—traumatic brain injury. It comes from getting shot in the head, or hitting the concrete with your skull, or from shock waves knocking your brain around when there's an explosion next to you and then your brain swells up. TBI. Who'd ever heard of it? It wasn't fair.

Ben had a long trip home. When he was hit, they took him to a field hospital and then they loaded him in the belly of a special plane that was fixed up for taking care of the wounded. They landed in Germany and held him in the hospital there for a couple of days to stabilize. Then they flew him to the military hospital in DC. Mom and Dad were already there, waiting for him in a motel an hour out of town. Dad called home every night and talked to Grandpa Roy about Ben, the ranch, Lali, and me. Mom couldn't hold it together enough to say more than, "Love you," or "I'll see you soon." Then you'd hear her voice crack, and she'd pass the phone back to Dad.

They weren't telling me much about what happened, so I went on the Internet and found pictures of the special plane. It was pretty cool how they set that up, but I couldn't see the wounded guys, so I found some blogs of soldiers who'd got shot up. They looked okay, sitting in their hospital beds, but some days I couldn't read all the way through their stories. One had had his feet blown off. Even so, he said he could feel them at night like they were still there. He hadn't slept for weeks. At least Ben had his feet.

Lali came in and I switched off the computer so she wouldn't see. "Cammy, teach me to ride Pretty."

"You can't ride that goat, silly. You'll get hurt."

"But I need to practice for the mutton busting at the fair. I want Ben to see me when he comes home."

"Then you should put a saddle on a sheep," I teased. But even Lali couldn't make me feel better after what I'd just read. I gave her a hug, grabbed my board, and biked over to Mike's.

That's where I always went when I felt rotten. Mike was the best. His folks moved them over from California when we were in third grade. He was the only new kid we had that year. His mom sent him to school in fancy clothes and new cowboy boots, like he'd need those at school. First thing he did was set his skateboard on his desk. So, Mrs. Lindsay took it away. Mike rolled his eyes around in a circle and stuck out his tongue lizard-style. Nobody else could do that, and I knew right then we'd be friends.

Mike and me used to play a lot of tricks. Like the time we built a catapult behind my house. We balanced an old plank on a rock like a teeter-totter and set a cantaloupe on one end. Mike jumped, hard as he could, on the other side.

"There it goes!" he yelled.

Then the melon landed, splat, in Mom's basket of clean laundry by the line.

"Oh man," I looked at him. "We're in trouble now." And we were. We had to wash up all that stuff and hang it out again, and we had to pick cantaloupes out of the garden for a week. But it was worth it to see that melon fly.

Mike's family, the Giannis, have a big house and a paved driveway, which is why we started skateboarding there. They let us build a skate ramp and keep it in their garage, and they put in floodlights just so we could practice at night. Mike's dad even set an iron rail into one side of the driveway so we could set the ramp next to it and slide on it. When we were in fifth grade, Mike and I made a promise. No matter what else happened, we'd skateboard together. It started when Mike broke his arm because he missed a landing and I rode with him to the emergency room.

"You guys should take it easy with the skating," the doctor said to him. "I see a lot of skateboard injuries."

"I keep telling him that," Mike's mom said. "I think you boys should take up basketball. Especially you, Cam, you're growing so tall."

Mike rolled his eyes. After he picked out his cast—red so we could draw cool skating logos on it—we rode home in the back of his mom's Lexus.

"You'll be back on your board soon," I said.

"Tomorrow," he answered.

"Absolutely not," his mother said.

Mike shook his head and stuck out his tongue, ducking so she couldn't see in the rearview mirror.

"We'll always be skaters," I said.

"Always," Mike said. "As long as we're friends." He rolled his good hand into a fist and reached toward me. We tapped our fists together to promise.

Now I pedaled as fast as I could, and when I got to Mike's house, he was already outside on his skateboard. There was a boarding jam coming up in Winnemucca, and Mike and I practiced together for it like we always did. Mike liked to call the tricks out and we'd do 'em. But now he could call out a bunch and I'd only remember the first one.

"What's up with you?" Mike asked. He wiped a smudge off his board with his T-shirt.

"Nothing," I said.

"We can't lose," he said. "I'm not losing 'cause you're going ADD on me."

"I can't stop thinking about Ben."

He ran his fingers through his hair. "Look, just skate. That's all you have to do."

"I'm trying."

He bopped me with his baseball cap and took off on his

skateboard. "You'll be okay. I know you. But everybody will be there watching, so focus, you dork."

"I'm good," I said. And I pumped up to speed and roared around his driveway. The dry air stung my face. My board felt solid under my feet, and when I took off the end of the ramp, I kept myself straight over it. I got good air, sailing high and long, and then all four wheels hit the ground with a deep thump. I flexed my knees to take the shock and turned toward Mike. "Focused enough?" I yelled at him. But as I coasted to a stop, I figured Mike might be right. We might lose 'cause I couldn't think straight anymore.

Boarding made the waiting bearable. That and Dad's calls. Ben was going to live, that was the first one. When we got the news, Grandpa Roy let out a whoop to curl your hair. Then Ben was awake, but when he came out of the coma, he couldn't talk. The doctors said his brain was like a clean slate. The brain injury had scrambled up the nerves in his brain. They thought he'd get them back to working better, but it needed time. He couldn't walk, either. But pretty soon he could sit up. Next he said a word: "Eat." I didn't want to think about Ben learning how to eat and talk again. He couldn't say what happened to him, although it had to do with an explosion. Two other guys who were with him died. "At least Ben's alive," Mom said. "The doctors work miracles. He'll be back to himself soon enough." She passed the phone to Dad, and he sprung it on me.

"Cam, I've got something to tell you. About Ben."

Of course it was about Ben. "What?" I asked.

"The doctors have done what they can for now. He's so much better than he was." There was a long silence on the line. I wanted to talk to fill it up, but I knew Dad wasn't done. "He's paralyzed."

"How paralyzed? Can they fix him?"

"Well, that's the good part. He can move his upper body, and he gets more control every day. It's an incomplete paralysis—his right leg and arm don't work. He can't stand yet, but he may. These brain injuries, they don't know how they'll turn out. It could get better with therapy. That's the good part."

Good part? This was good? "So will he be able to walk?"

Dad swallowed and it echoed on the phone line. "That doesn't look good yet," he said. "But he can move his upper body."

"You said that," I said. "I don't believe it. The doctors are wrong. He'll walk, he will." Then my throat backed up, and I passed the phone to Grandpa.

There's this thing that happens when I'm sad. Colors fade and rooms close in on themselves. Everything turns, well, gray. Waiting for Ben was so long and muddled, I call it the gray time. And it would have choked me except Grandma Jean showed up.

✳ CHAPTER ✳

FIVE

Dad calls Grandma Jean a loose cannon, but I just love her to death. Nobody has a better grandma than I do. And no, she isn't any relation to Grandpa Roy, except because her daughter married his son. Grandpa Roy is Dad's dad and Grandma Jean is my mom's mother. Her last name is Carl, and Dad and Grandpa and the rest of us are O'Maras. So they're on either side of the family, and man, are those sides different. Grandma Jean's about the only one who could make me laugh in the gray time. I'm thankful she did.

She drove up from Hawthorne. It took her thirty-six hours to get the news, pack her beat-up fire-engine red Ford Bronco, and drive the five hours to Salt Lick. She brought clothes for a month, licorice for Lali, and the heat. It hit ninety-seven the day she arrived, with more predicted.

"Good night! Have you three been moping around here since it happened?" she asked, including Grandpa Roy in her scolding. "It doesn't help, you know." She put on a Reba

McIntyre CD and turned up the volume. Next, she opened the windows to let the fresh air blow in. She passed the time under the yellow-splattered cottonwoods out front. She filled Lali's wading pool, put in a lawn chair, and brought out her romance novels.

"It seems to me everybody around here's talking about Ben like he's dead already."

"I can't believe you just said that," I blurted out.

Lali jumped in the pool and splashed Grandma Jean, and Grandma splashed her right back. She wiped some drops off of the cover of her novel. "Well, we'll give 'em something *else* to talk about. We will tonight." She grinned at me.

I knew that look. Your grandma probably isn't like mine, unless she's always playing tricks and jokes on people. Ben might be suffering and Mom and Dad gone back east, but Grandma Jean, she stayed the same.

About the time most people were going to bed, she started the dishwasher and handed me a flashlight.

"Roy, you'll watch Lali while Cam and I run an errand, won't you?"

"I always do. What business have you got going out at this hour?" He looked from her to me and back again. "No, don't tell me. I don't want to know." He picked up the TV remote and settled into the couch. Grandma Jean disappeared into her room and came out with her purse.

It was a cloth bag with round wooden handles and red roses all over it. Not that there was one thing about Grandma Jean that would make you think of roses, but the bag, which she was proud to say she bought for next to nothing at a swap meet, was enormous and she liked that.

It was a mystery what Grandma could hide in there—books, knitting, chocolate bars, and the like.

Some of her stuff was strange. She carried a baby picture of my cousin Adam Carl, who drowned on his ninth birthday. She said he was our guardian angel now, and she wouldn't leave the house without his picture. And she kept a little red plastic pouch with a couple of strands of his baby hair, some sage leaves, some salt from out to our salt lick, and a medal of St. Jude—the saint for lost causes—that one of her friends gave her. She carried all that just so Adam could find us. She made one like it for Ben when he went overseas too. "A little extra insurance, in case that O'Mara luck wasn't enough"—a lot of good it did him. Grandma's rose bag was always bulging, so who knew what else she'd stuffed in there. She nodded to me and the two of us climbed into her Bronco.

A sliver of moon slid behind Sugar Peak as Grandma drove down Main Street. The only other people around were in the bar on the far end of the street. The single streetlight hadn't had a bulb since Tom Lehi, a gold miner who'd been around here for sixty of his ninety years, got tired of it and shot it out. Floating in that darkness, the stars seemed close enough to grab.

"Like I told you, this town needs something else to talk about," Grandma said. "You children don't need folks creeping around talking about your brother like he was a cripple and whispering behind your back." She stopped the car in front of the closed-down antique store and motioned for me to get out.

"So let's change the subject, so to speak," Grandma Jean said. "Turn on that flashlight."

I held the flashlight while Grandma opened her handbag and laid out a length of ¾-inch irrigation tubing, scissors, two irrigation joints, a Laundromat-sized box of detergent, and a packet of powdered orange-drink mix in the back of the Bronco.

"What are we doing?" I asked.

"We're fixing that fountain," Grandma said seriously. She nodded toward a plaster fountain that Mike's mom had stuck front and center by the walk to the antique store—to spruce things up. I always thought it looked silly to have Roman cherubs playing in the water out in central Nevada. 'Specially since the water line froze and busted the first winter, leaving them dancing in the dust.

I didn't know Grandma's plan, exactly, but I knew what the irrigation stuff was for, so I found the broken water line, cut the bad part out, and jammed the joints onto each open end. I cut a patch from Grandma's line and stuck the ends into the joints. The line was connected to the store by a garden hose and an orange electric cord ran the pump. Grandma Jean turned the spigot and started the water. "Tell me when it's full," she said.

I watched the fountain bowl fill up beneath the pair of plaster cherubs that balanced above it. "It's full," I whispered.

Grandma brushed the spiderwebs off the outlet by the outside fuse box and plugged in the cord. The pump churned on. Water spewed from the cherubs mouths. I started to giggle. Then I really laughed.

"What's funny?" Grandma asked.

"It looks like they're throwing up."

Grandma cackled. "Just wait."

She poured the detergent into the bowl and nodded to me to add the orange powder. "We're on our way," Grandma said. "That should hold 'em for a while."

The next morning, it was the talk of the school and the town. Someone had started up that crazy fountain and filled it with bubbly orange detergent. The stuff oozed out all over Main Street, and the cherubs drooled orange goo all day. No one knew who did it. Only Grandpa Roy could guess it was me and my grandma Jean.

Dad came home alone in mid-September. Ben needed more time in the hospital back east, but Dad had to get back to the ranch. Mom got a leave from her job at the bank in Winnemucca and took a room in the house the military keeps for families of wounded guys. She said she'd stay till they moved Ben out to rehab, maybe in California.

I can't tell you how disappointed Grandpa Roy was. He'd been counting the days till Ben was "safe at home where he belongs." He took to spending more time in the barn than not. One day after school, I went out to find him. I didn't see Grandpa, so I picked up a soft horse brush and talked to my colt. "You think we'll win the skateboard competition? Sure you do. And what about Ben, you think he'll learn to walk, don't you?" The colt leaned against me and nosed in my pocket for grain.

I heard someone behind me. I turned and thought I saw Grandpa's shadow move across the entrance to the barn, but I didn't see him. "Grandpa, you there?" I called.

"Yep," Grandpa said. He cleared his throat and walked out of the tack room on the other side of the barn. "I heard you talking about Ben. 'Course he'll walk again. He's an O'Mara. He's a champ. Here, let me see how you've got this colt leading." Grandpa took a halter from the wall and guided it around the colt's nose. He pulled the horse's ears through and buckled the chin strap.

"You believe Ben will ride again in the rodeos, don't you?" I asked.

"I believe those military doctors don't know who they're dealing with. Ben O'Mara's one stubborn boy. Yeah, I believe he'll talk and walk and make a nuisance of himself, just like always. And if he don't . . . well . . . I thought there'd be another O'Mara champion, though. That boy has bulls in his blood. Strange how things work out. I couldn't have been prouder when he joined the service. Who'd have thought he'd come back. . . ." Grandpa Roy handed me the lead rope. He cleared his throat again, pulled his hat down across his forehead, and left the barn.

That's how it is with Grandpa Roy and my dad, too. That side of the family, they stop talking midsentence if it suits them. Pouring detergent into a fountain isn't their style. They just take it as it comes, and if it's too tough, they bite down hard and take some more. Me, I couldn't figure a way to stop worrying while we waited for Ben. And when I wasn't tied up in knots thinking about him, I got mad that he went and got shot and took all the attention again. Grandma Jean would call those ugly thoughts, and I had to agree. I was thinking way too much—so I studied less and boarded more.

My grades started down, and Favi stepped up to help me. That was no surprise. Her family and mine, Ruizes and O'Maras, have worked our ranch together since my dad was a kid. It takes two or three families and some extra ranch hands to run a ranch like ours. We all help each other and nobody gets rich. My mom had a job at the bank in Winnemucca, and Favi's mom was the kindergarten teacher at school. Dad and Grandpa and Oscar Ruiz worked the ranch. Ben was a natural ranch hand, and me and Favi and her sisters, when they still lived at home, helped too. Even Lali took care of the goats and had her egg and chicken chores. Still, there's never extra money, and if there ever was a little, Grandpa and Dad usually bought some new equipment or reroofed a barn.

That's how we live—with the land. And with family. That included Favi. She acted like a sister, too, ordering me around when I could decide just fine for myself. That's what she did to help me study for our English vocabulary test.

"So give me the definition of 'intrepid,'" she said.

"I know what 'cataclysmic' means," I answered her.

"Not relevant," Favi said. "Do you want to pass this test or not?"

"Yeah, I want to pass the test," I said. Mom was strict about grades and I'd be busted for sure if she came back and I'd let them slip. "Tell me what it means."

"You look it up, Cam. I'm not doing everything for you."

"I didn't ask you to."

"You didn't need to. You always take the easy way."

"Who died and made you queen?"

Favi gave me that look of hers. She'd lift one eyebrow just enough to let you know she was wondering why you ever said what you just said. She shoved a dictionary at me and I paged through it looking for "intrepid."

"Good," she said. "How's Ben?"

"Mom hasn't called today."

"She will. I bet Ben's having a good day and she's still at the hospital." How she could beat everybody at school at video games, get herself greasy working under her dad's car, and then turn around and say just the right thing, I'll never know.

We finished and Favi walked back to her house. I talked Grandma Jean into driving me to Mike's to board. Lali tagged along. Grandma pulled up to Mike's, and I jumped out with my skateboard. We set up our ramps, and Lali ran around back with Mike's dog. Grandma Jean sat down on the porch just like she lived there, and Mrs. Gianni came out with coffee. "It's too bad about Ben," Mrs. Gianni said.

"He'll be fine," Grandma said.

"Well, it's such a loss, a young kid in the military like that, he was so strong. . . . And the whole town couldn't have been prouder of his bull riding."

I used the drone of the board's wheels to block out their talk. While Mike warmed up, I coasted down the driveway, ollied onto the ledge, and did a 50-50, sliding my board along the edge until I kicked off. Then I sped up, hit the ramp, and landed dead center on the metal rail, spraying sparks. I wobbled and jumped off. "Man, I never hit that."

"Practice makes perfect," Grandma Jean said.

I rolled my eyes at Mike. "Let's try our routine."

Mike called out the tricks. We started at each end of the driveway, met in the middle, and did frontside flips at the same time. We landed the first one. On the second pass, we switched to 360s. Mike leaned too far back on the landing and ended up on his back. Then I hit a bump on the driveway and drove my elbow into the asphalt.

"Stay on your feet!" Mike yelled at me.

"I'll get it down before the skate jam," I said. I picked up my board and walked past the porch to start over.

"I wish they didn't crash so much," Mrs. Gianni said. "Ever since Mike broke his arm, in two places you know, I can hardly watch."

"Heavens, you should go to a rodeo," Grandma Jean said. "There's some bruising goes on there."

But there was nothing in skateboarding or rodeo to get me ready for the licking Ben had taken in Iraq. They moved him to Palo Alto at the end of September to a TBI rehabilitation unit at the Veteran's Hospital. Mom flew to California with him. He could talk some now, and he even called me. "Hi, Cam." His voice was slurred. "How's skateboarding?"

"Good," I said. "How are you?"

"Mom takes me dancing." He made a sound I took for a laugh.

"Yeah, right. When do you come home?" I asked.

"Leave. They give me leave. Ask Ma." He faded out, and Mom came on the line.

"Isn't he talking great?" she asked.

I thought he sounded awful—like he was drunk. "Sure," I said. "When are you coming home?"

"It shouldn't be too long. They'll give him a thirty-day leave when the doctors here think he's ready. They need to make sure I can take care of him. We're working on that. I miss you, Cam."

I missed her too. By early October, the doctors had done all their tests, and they said Ben was ready to start his rehab. But first he got leave. The gray time was over. Ben came home.

SIX

If you just could have seen my brother before. He was wiry and strong, with a quick smile like my mom's. He never left Salt Lick but he slicked himself up in a pressed shirt and clean jeans. The girls all followed him with their eyes. Even my friends wanted to hang out with Ben, and now that he was coming home, Favi showed up and walked in without knocking. "Hey, Cam," she said. Then she picked up Lali and swung her around.

"Isn't this going to be so cool?" she said. "Aren't you excited? Ben's been gone for months and now he's almost home." She reached in the fridge and took out a carrot. She snapped it in half and gave a piece to Lali, then crunched down on the big end she had left.

"Do you want a pop?" I asked her.

She didn't bother to answer.

So all of us hung out—Grandpa Roy, Grandma Jean, Lali, me, and Favi—until we heard the motor on Dad's truck. Lali grabbed the dog and jumped up and down on the porch. I leaned against the cherry tree—it looked cool and it would hold me steady. I was shaking.

I peered into the Ford F-250 as it rumbled up the driveway, but I couldn't see Ben. I realized he must be lying down on the cramped backseat. Mom was turned clear around, talking to him. Dad stopped, jumped out of the truck, and jogged around to the back. Grandpa met him from the other side.

"Ben!" Lali called. She ran to the truck, climbed up on the running board and pressed her nose against the window.

"Give him some room, pumpkin," Grandpa Roy said.

Together, Dad and Grandpa lifted out a wheelchair and then a rented hospital bed. I dug my heels in and pressed my back to the tree. Man, they were bringing in a whole hospital ward.

I backtracked into the house and pulled my board out from under the bed. Our driveway wasn't paved like Mike's, but our patio was big and concrete. I went out the back door and pushed around in long circles. I heard them all talking. There was hustling and bumping. They were moving the bed in—and Ben. I glanced at the window and then turned the other way. I pumped my foot faster. The wheels roared, louder than their conversation. It was like balancing on the crossbar of a fence. I wanted to jump down, and I wanted to stay on top. Ben was inside, but my legs wouldn't let me go in to see him.

"Cam," Mom called, "come on and say hello. We're all here now, Cam." I took a breath and kicked my board up into my hand. I could manage this, I told myself. I put a little grin on my face and walked through the back door. The living room was cramped with the hospital bed propped upright next to Mom's piano. Ben was facing away from me, in a wheelchair. He wore a blue plastic padded helmet that looked like the kind boxers wear, but aside from that, from this angle he looked the same. My heart raced. "Hey, Ben," I said.

Grandpa Roy turned the wheelchair around so Ben could see me. I stopped dead. They hadn't told me. He wasn't just shot. His left arm was gone below the elbow. Instead of a hand, he had a metal hook. He had a red, welty scar running up his neck that stopped just below his chin. He smiled at me with his mouth, but his eyes looked tired. "No. No." I covered my mouth to stop the words. *No. Not my brother.* They'd gone and blown him up.

I escaped into the kitchen and Grandma Jean followed me.

"Cam . . ." She just took my hand. Hers was cold. I couldn't look at her. She squeezed my hand and went back to join the family.

I called Mike. "I'm coming down to skateboard."

"Don't you want to be there when Ben comes home?" he asked.

"He is here, and I'm leaving. He's got Mom and Dad and the whole family with him. I need to get out of here."

"Okay, no worries. I just thought you'd want to be with your brother. I didn't mean you had to stick around," Mike said.

"It's a mess and I'd rather board. Meet me at the Grange."

The Grange had a parking lot, and although we didn't have ramps or anything there, it was halfway between our houses and you could get up some speed on the asphalt. I needed speed. I picked up my board and started out the back door, but Favi stopped me.

"Where are you going? Ben wants to see you," she said.

"I doubt it," I said. "You see him."

"Come on, Cam, you have to stay. You've been waiting so long for him to get home. You'll hurt his feelings."

"Naw, he won't care."

"You know he will, Cam. This is *important*."

"I'm meeting Mike," I said. I walked past her.

"You little baby. What do you know? Put that board down and stay or I'm telling your mom."

I might have stayed too, if she hadn't called me little and a baby. I kept going and didn't look back. No one came after me either.

Mike was at the Grange, waiting for me.

"So, why aren't you home?"

I pushed my board around the lot. The wheels got louder and louder. Mike threw his Oakland A's cap at me. "Answer me at least," he said.

I jumped off the board. "You haven't seen him. They didn't tell me what happened. He's not the same. He's not Ben."

"You knew he was messed up," Mike said.

"But it's different seeing him. Besides, they're all mooning around him and they won't miss me."

Mike didn't talk any more. That's what makes him cool—he shuts up when he needs to. We kept boarding until the sun dipped into the willow trees and the fall chill pulled goose bumps out of my skin. Then my mom drove into the lot. She rolled down the window.

"Come on home, Cam."

I skated slower.

"It's dinnertime and I need you home. Ben wants to talk to you."

"About what?" I asked, still pushing myself enough to make her drive along next to me.

"About things. He's worried about you."

"He's got his own stuff to worry about."

"That's exactly right, so come on." She stopped the car and opened the door. I picked up my board and got in.

"You're a big guy, Cam. You can handle this."

"You and Dad lied about him," I said.

"We didn't lie. We just didn't tell you everything. We didn't know how much he'd heal, how much the doctors could fix. We thought for a while they could save his arm. And we didn't want to worry you and Lali. You were just starting a new school year."

"Lali's a baby, I'm not. You should have said."

"Maybe. Everything happened so fast, Cam. Dad and I just had to get through each day. But that's over now. Come home and be his brother. He needs you."

Now that was something to think on. Ben never needed anything, and if he did, he didn't say. I'm guessing he didn't like needing stuff, and that he didn't like sitting in a wheelchair or wearing a helmet or needing his little brother. And you know, I didn't like it much either.

When we got home, it was almost dark and everyone but Ben was clearing the table and working on the dinner dishes. Mom pointed me in the direction of the living room. They'd fixed Ben's hospital bed in the middle of the room, and he was asleep. The helmet was on the coffee table. Part of his head was shaved, and it was dented in like you'd pushed your palm into bread dough. It throbbed with his pulse. I watched him breathe for a while. Then, he opened his eyes and gave me a real smile. "Sit down," he said, patting the bed.

I reached for a chair and he patted the bed again. "Are you sure it's okay?" I asked.

"Yeah. You can't hurt me more." He almost laughed.

I sat as close to the edge of the bed as I could. I didn't want to bump him. "So, can you walk?"

"They think, maybe. Later."

I looked at him for a while. "Does it hurt?"

"I get big headaches, and," he pointed to his arm and said, "that hurts."

I tried not to look at his stump or to stare at his head. "Were you scared?" I asked. While Ben was in Iraq, I tried not to think of the twisted cars or blown-out buildings they showed on the news. In fact, sometimes I pretended he wasn't over there. But now I was asking, "How did it feel when . . . that . . . happened?"

He started slow. He had to search around for his words, and as he talked they came to him even slower. "No time for scared," he said. "Gone weapons searching, then." He stopped again. "Bang," he said, and turned his head. "This awful bad smell. Noise. Real loud. Gunshots are loud, Cam, but this was huge." He paused again. "I can't remember. That's maybe good." He looked back and forth around the room.

"Ben, are you okay?"

"Okay? You think I'm okay? See what they did to me? The noise . . ." He thrashed around, trying to sit up like he was going to take a swing at me and then he fell back onto the pillow. "Well, I'm here, right? I could be dead." He gave me a big grin. "Here is better." He looked at the ceiling and sunk deeper into the bed. "Cam, I can't do . . . walk . . . It's scary."

I flexed my own thigh muscles, just to feel how that worked, and I hoped Ben hadn't seen it.

"So, do you remember what hit you?" I asked.

"IED—explosion. It blew me up, huh? Mom can tell you."

"I hate them for blowing you up."

"Hate's a big word, bro'."

I choked up when he called me bro'. It was so hard for him to put the words together, but he got that one. *Bro'.* "Well, don't you hate them? Don't you just want to go back over there and kill all those guys 'cause they did this to you?"

"Don't know who to kill. And they already got me." He touched his arm. It gave me the willies. "But no, I don't hate them. They got their job and I got mine," he said. He paused and added, "I just wasn't so lucky."

CHAPTER

SEVEN

I'm guessing you haven't lived with someone who's been shot up. There's a good piece of discomfort and awkwardness when there's someone in the house, someone you love, who can't do for himself. Ben needed help getting dressed on account of his arm, and getting in and out of bed on account of the paralysis in his right leg. Mom flexed his feet and legs every so often, so the muscles wouldn't just fade away. We had to help him move so he didn't sit too long in any one position—his skin could get sore and break. And there was the wheelchair.

But the worst was the bathroom. He didn't want any help in there, but, like I said, he was pretty messed up. And we didn't have a shower downstairs, so he had to wash up in the sink. Ben would disappear into the bathroom and stay until you could just about feel his exhaustion. Then Mom would knock on the door to go in to help, but it embarrassed him. And her too, I think. They'd both come out quiet. Mom would move Ben's wheelchair by the window, and he'd stare out while she got real busy in the rest of the house. We tried not to notice, but you really couldn't help it, especially if you were waiting for the bathroom and had to go pee outside. Still, no one talked about it. And then, one day, Grandpa Roy, went to the bathroom door instead of Mom. You could hear him talking to Ben in there, and then they were both laughing. When Grandpa Roy wheeled Ben out, he set him on the porch and pulled up a chair next to him.

"The calves put on good weight over the summer. The grass was good. This fall bunch should be healthy too," he said.

"How many calves?" Ben asked.

And just like that, Grandpa Roy took over as Ben's caretaker. We all relaxed a notch. Grandpa Roy, he was more like Ben's brother than I was, I guess. And he wasn't a woman, which helped some too.

And there were other things. The house always smelled of medicine. Lali stopped playing catch with me outside and started sitting next to Ben. Since his brain had been scrambled up, he had to relearn how to read. So she read him comic books and her favorite picture books and he followed along. Some days he couldn't string three words together, and other days he talked pretty good. And you never knew what he could remember. Mom got out the photo albums and left them around so we could point out stuff to Ben that we'd done.

"Remember going to Sea World?" she asked.

Ben looked at her blankly.

"We all went. Except Lali. She wasn't born yet. Remember, you loved the killer whale show?"

Ben nodded, but you could tell that he didn't remember it. I turned on the TV so he didn't have to embarrass himself any more.

That's how it went. Mom worked long hours starting up a bookkeeping business, since the bank wouldn't hold her job anymore, and with Grandpa Roy helping Ben, Dad always had extra work around the ranch. There wasn't money to hire another hand, although Ruiz had offered to take a cut in his pay. Dad said no to that, so I had more chores too.

One Saturday, in mid-October, Grandma Jean was bored. "Roy, it's blasted quiet around here," she said. "We should take these kids on an outing."

"You want to go fishing? They're getting good walleye at Rye Patch."

"You'd scare the fish away with your old face," she said. "Let's go into Winnemucca and get some ice cream and see a movie."

I didn't want to see a movie with my little sister and my grandparents. "I can stay here," I said.

"I'd rather fish," Grandpa Roy said. "You take Lali and go. You can see a kids' movie."

Lali clapped her hands. Grandma Jean got her rose-covered handbag, and they went off to the movies. Mom was gone over at Mike's, doing the accounts for Gianni's Irrigation and Plumbing. Dad, Oscar Ruiz, and a couple of ranch hands were clearing debris with the front loader. That left me, Ben, and Grandpa Roy in the house.

"We should get out too," Grandpa said.

"Then why didn't you go to the movies?"

"That's no place for Ben, and you want to come too, don't you?" he said to my brother.

Ben frowned and said, "No."

"Of course you do. You haven't been anywhere but out on the porch since we planted you in the living room. It's done then." When he said that, there'd be no arguing. Ben couldn't claim paralysis or pain or anything else. He'd just wait for his orders from Grandpa.

"Where we going?" I asked, looking for my own instructions.

"The bull ring."

Wow. What do you know? Grandpa Roy was still fixed on getting Ben to the bull ring, crippled or not.

"I don't want to," Ben snapped.

"You need to see those boys sometime, and Darrell called and told me they've got some new bucking bulls they're trying out. They brought 'em in from Elko. Come on, Cam. Help me get Ben in the chair."

"I'm not going," Ben said. "I'm not s'posed to go out."

"Sure you are," Grandpa answered. He reached for Ben's helmet.

"No helmet. Not there," he said. He looked desperate.

"Get his hat, Cam. You'll go cowboy-like today."

Now, Ben wasn't supposed to take unnecessary trips, and the rule was that he had to wear his helmet anytime he moved somewhere. It protected the hole they'd cut in his skull to let his brain swell out of his head when he was first injured. But Grandpa Roy was breaking the rules. I fetched Ben's cowboy hat. Then Grandpa took Ben's shattered arm and motioned for me to get his good one. Ben groaned when Grandpa touched his stump, but he flexed his elbow and bore weight on his upper arm. He bit his lip and helped us move him the best he could. We held on and he tensed his upper body, and we swung him, stiff-like, into the wheelchair. His good arm and elbow felt hard and warm against my hands. He was like an iron man above the waist. There was no thinking he was a kid or even a teenager anymore, although he was nineteen. When I pivoted Ben into his chair, I was moving a man.

We did the same drill at the truck. Grandpa drove it up close to the porch where Dad had knocked out a railing. The porch and the cab were almost level, so we could move Ben onto the seat without lifting much. We got him in, and I ran to the other side and climbed in next to him. Grandpa straightened his hat and started the truck. Now, the roads from the ranch to the bull ring are mostly dirt and gravel. And they have enough holes and washboarding to give you a good jarring unless you go fast. So Grandpa hit the gas and I pushed up against Ben enough that he wouldn't bounce around, and he held on to the door with his only hand.

It was a bright day and fall was in full swing. The rabbitbrush was fuzzy with yellow blooms, and the willows were already half-bare. We crossed Salt Creek where the water tumbled through the rocks, ice cold from October's overnight snows and afternoon melts in the high country. Ben rolled down the window and let the wind come through. Grandpa was right. It felt good to get out.

There was a bunch of trucks and trailers already round the bull ring. You could tell where the animals were, in the pen behind the arena, by the dust they raised. And, as always, there were cowboys hanging out, talking and giving advice, and there were cowboys working on their bull ropes because they intended to skip the advice and just ride. I can't tell you how many times I'd been here. When I was real little and it was Dad riding, I was one of the kids who played hide-and-seek around the trucks or carried gear and water to the riders. Later, when Dad took over more chores from Grandpa on the ranch, it was Ben riding. At the bull ring, I was always Ben's little brother, or Dad's kid, or Roy's little guy. Today, I figured I'd be less than that. All eyes were on the truck, waiting for Ben.

Grandpa Roy pulled in, dropped the gear shift into first, and slid out of the truck in one smooth motion. He went to the back and pulled out Ben's wheelchair. The men gave him space, holding themselves at a respectful distance and turning enough to see but not to stare. Grandpa opened the door. I got behind Ben on the seat and put my hands under his armpits. Grandpa took his hips and we lowered him to the running board. Then, a couple of Ben's friends broke out of the group and jogged over to help. One held the chair and the other one worked with Grandpa to get Ben off the truck and eased into the wheelchair. I couldn't see Ben's face under his hat, but his hand tensed up on the arm of the chair and the veins stood out.

Darrell Wallace said, "Hey, Ben." He knelt down to get eye level with Ben. "It's good to see you, man." His voice trembled.

Ben took his hand.

"Okay, then." Darrell jumped up, grabbed the chair,

tipped it back, and spun it around. "Let's see if you can do eight seconds in this," he said. "What took you so long? We figured you'd just crawl over to see us if you had to. I never knew you to be away from the bulls for more than a day. So why you ignoring us?"

Ben reached back with his hand and grabbed Darrell's again. He held it for a few seconds, squeezing. Then he pushed his hat back, smiled, though his face was flushed, and said as clear as I'd heard him talk since he'd been home, "I figured you guys was too mean . . . and ugly. And I'm already broke. Don't need no bull . . . to do it again."

Andrew Echevarria came over. He and Darrell were the only ones around here who could beat Ben in the ring—sometimes. "Well, we could tie you on and see if you stick. Some of these yahoos would like to try that themselves."

Darrell pushed the chair toward the ring. The men made a knot around Ben, talking and asking questions. Ben answered as best he could and laughed. Grandpa and I tagged behind, tasting the dust they kicked up. They parked Ben parallel to the chute. This wasn't a pro ring, with its six chutes and fancy advertisements hanging on the gates. It was a one-chute deal, with a couple of holding pens in the back. The men took turns helping the rider flank and rope the bull, settling him in the chute, and playing bullfighter when he got thrown. Most days nobody kept time, but when there was a jackpot or a bet on the line, then the timer wasn't a big digital clock, but Grandpa Roy or some other old guy with a stopwatch. There was nothing fancy about the Salt Lick bull ring except the wins these cowboys made. Salt Lick had its share of winners.

SUZANNE MORGAN WILLIAMS

I realized I hadn't been here myself since Ben left for the Marines. If I looked at Ben just the right way, I could forget the wheelchair and pretend he was home on his last leave, getting ready to ride himself. I closed my eyes and replayed Dad's tape of Ben's championship ride in my mind. I smelled the manure and the sage and fixed on the sun warming my back. It felt good.

"Cam, check out . . . the bulls," Ben called. "Tell me—can Darrell stick on one?" He laughed some more.

I walked past Ben and climbed the rails by the chute for a better look. There were four smallish long-horned bulls and a big Brahma in the holding pen. "I'd put him on the little red one," I said. "That looks like his speed."

Darrell shouted, "The kid's got a sense of humor. That looks more like your bull, Cam O'Mara."

"No bull is my bull," I said. "I'll take you on at the skate park, though."

"And I'd beat you there, same as here," Darrell said.

"Don't think so," Ben said. "You should . . . see him skateboard."

"Well, I think it's time to see him on a bull." Darrell mussed my hair. I pushed his hand away. "It's time you live up to that O'Mara name your daddy gave you."

"I don't ride," I said again.

"When you're ready, you let me know. We'll go head-to-head, bull to board. And I'll win."

"'Course you will," one of the men said. "The kid's only in junior high."

I looked at Ben and Grandpa. They were laughing, but I didn't know what was so funny.

"Come here, squirt," Darrell kept at it. "I'll just set you on the little red one. He's a steer, you know. Comes along as companion to that big black Brahma, Quicksand. He'll be a good one for you 'cause he's sweet."

One part of me wanted to puff up and say, *Give me the big, black one*, but even the little steer looked huge to me. Steers, cows, bulls, don't matter, they all look pretty tall when you get up next to them. But more than that, I wanted to say, *No thanks, I'm a skateboarder.* Before I said either, Darrell started messing with me again.

"I guess Ben was the bull rider in the family. It's a shame he got you for a little sister."

Now that was it. You can tease me, and you can say I'm in junior high when I've started ninth grade and am tall enough to look you in the eye. You can call me a skater wimp like Ben used to do, but man, don't add slams about the O'Mara name and then call me a girl. Even if you are Ben's buddy. I turned to look at Ben and Grandpa standing right behind him, and neither one of them was laughing now. Grandpa wet his lips and nodded his head, slow, so I'd get the message. And then Ben tossed his hat at me. It landed short on account of his right arm was still gimpy. "Let's go, bro'," he said. Grandpa set his own hat on Ben, covering up the dent in his skull.

So, instead of making an excuse, like a sane person, I put on Ben's hat and pulled it down tight across my forehead. Darrell took off his protective vest—it was hard inside to keep a bull from stomping your middle—and handed it to me. I zipped it on, trying not to shake. And one foot after another, I climbed up the rails to the narrow platform behind the chutes. Up there, wearing Ben's hat, I felt like we were back to being brothers for the first time since he'd come home.

They said the steer's name was Possum 'cause it could look half-dead and then wake right up. I was rooting for the half-dead style. Andrew picked up his bull rope and moved Possum into the bucking chute. Rodeo chutes can look like a maze of metal rails, but they're simple contraptions. Each chute has four sides—just bull-size. The back end slides out to let the bull in, and then a cowboy pushes it closed behind him. The bull rider, that was me, perches alongside the chute on a platform that's level with the top of the railings. When it's time to get on the bull, he swings across the rails and lowers himself onto the bull's back. The long side of the chute is hinged to open into the arena. Say the word and they let the animal go. That's it. Simple. Unless you've decided to be the cowboy on top of the bull.

Possum walked into the chute and one of the guys slid the gate behind him. It was time to put on the bull rope. Now, the pro bull riders and the bigger rodeos, they have a special rigging chute that makes the whole deal a lot easier. But in a little hometown arena like we had in Salt Lick, we made do with the fish-and-stretch method: dangle the rope down one side of the chute and a second cowboy on the other side of the chute reaches a long wire hook under the bull to catch the rope. Work both sides of the bull rope up to the top of the chute and stretch across the bull to pull it around him like a ribbon on a package. That's how they rigged up Possum. And all the while the steer was moving back and forth into the sides of the chute. With every bang, the whole chute moved. I could feel the size of him under my boots on the platform before I ever went over the rail.

I'd seen this a thousand times, and I knew that, since I was going to ride, or at least try to ride, the steer, I should be the one to fix the bull rope. But I didn't. I let Andrew reach in and adjust the size of the rope so it fit around the steer. He moved it back and forth until the handle was on top. I watched. And prayed.

I thought about jumping around and slapping my hands together like some guys do before they ride, but I felt quiet, so I waited till they tied the flank rope on Possum. That's when you have to decide. And I'm telling you, you have to decide every time. Are you going over the rails to get on the bull, or are you going to be smart and go back down? My instinct was to climb down. But Ben was watching me and then Darrell handed me his buckskin glove. I slipped it on my right hand and clenched my fingers, feeling the pine tar that bull riders rub on their gloves for extra grip stick my fingers together. Possum banged back and forth in the chute. I shivered.

"We'll ease you down," Darrell said. He put a hand under my armpit the same way I had put mine under Ben's to get him out of the truck, and right then, I swallowed, swung my legs across the rails, and dropped onto Possum.

The steer let go with a shower of poop. No offense meant, but the back end of a bull is pretty much a manure factory, and when they get excited it shoots everywhere. Even a little steer like Possum has a broad back. I stretched my legs out across him, settled in, and felt his muscles tense. "Hang on tight with them legs," Andrew said. He pulled the rope snug to cinch it on the steer. I was sure this animal didn't like me. "That feel good to you?" he asked. I didn't have a clue what felt good, but I nodded. "Now rough your rope." I ran my glove up and down the bull rope a bunch of times to raise the fuzz up and give me anything extra to hold on to. Then I slipped my hand into the handle, palm up. Andrew laid the tail of the rope across my fingers one direction, made a loop, and brought it back the other way on top of my palm. I wrapped my fingers around the rope, and Darrell reached in and squeezed my hand shut over the rope to seal everything up with the pine tar. The steer jumped to one side.

"Keep your toes in," Grandpa Roy yelled. I looked up and he was straddling the fence above me. I turned my left toe under the steer just before he would have ripped it along the rails. He jammed my knee into the boards instead, and I bit my lip to keep from yelling. This was when a clear thinker should have got out.

"Now sit forward when you ride," Grandpa said. "And don't forget your shoulders. Keep 'em square. You ready?" His face was taut with excitement. I felt the bull squash my leg and scrape it along the side of the chute.

"Ready," I said. They opened the chute wide, the steer jumped to the right, and I blacked out.

✦ **CHAPTER** ✦

EIGHT

Now in case you think I'm a wimp or something, I'm telling you a lot of the guys black out their first ride. That's what Ben says, anyway. There's just too much happening all at once. I don't think I stuck two seconds. I don't remember. I do remember scrambling up the rail and Possum trotting around the far end of the ring, with Andrew shooing him away from me. And from the throbbing, I can tell you I landed hard on my right side.

I brushed myself off and then I saw the cowboys watching me. "That's one way to ride a bull!" someone yelled. Everybody laughed.

"Well, he's lucky he passed out before he got a load of your ugly face," another one called.

I blushed and pulled Ben's hat down lower. I wished they were talking about anybody but me. I unzipped Darrell's vest and took it over to him. The odd thing was, when my head cleared enough to think, I was tingly and tight and wired and pumped up all at once. All I wanted was to do it again. But the guys were still joking about my ride, and getting on another steer meant I had to lower myself into the chute, and I was scared. Stomach-churning scared.

So I sat on the fence and tried to act cool, like blacking out on the back of a steer happened to me every day. Meanwhile, Darrell got settled for his ride. He picked the big black Brahma. Andrew pulled the gate clear back and, man, that bull shot out. He bucked high and landed four-footed, turned right, and then threw his head back, then ducked it to the left. Darrell went flying off to the side. He hit, bounced, and jumped to his feet, hopping one, two, three, four. He sprang up the fence like a jack rabbit and landed next to me.

"So, you gonna be a bull rider like your brother?"

"That's a lot of bull riding," I said.

"Yeah, it is," Darrell said, catching his breath. "But he's out and it seems like we could use another O'Mara in."

I stared at him to see if he was fooling with me after all that ribbing. But his face was serious the way guys are when they need you to believe something important.

"*Ben* and you are the bull riders," I said. Then I realized just how stupid that sounded now.

He took off his cowboy hat and wiped his forehead with the back of his hand. "Ben just goes with bull riding, don't he?" He knocked the dust off his hat. "Well, if it's not Ben, maybe it'll be you—someday. In or out?" he asked.

I jumped off the fence. "Let's see you on a board first."

"That's a bet, Cam O'Mara—you didn't do so good on the bulls, and I'll beat you at skateboarding, too."

"I'll take any bet you've got. Just show up," I said, grinning.

"Soon," he said.

"You're on."

Monday morning, Mike, Favi, and me sat together on the school bus. I was bursting to tell them about the bull riding, but Mike beat me to it, in the news category.

"My mom's been fainting again. This weird Meniere's Disease makes her ears ring and she loses her balance. They can't get her medications right."

"Is she going to be okay?" Favi asked.

"Yeah, the doctors aren't worried, but she can't drive for a while."

"That's too bad," Favi said.

"Too bad for her. My dad says he's got some big irrigation contracts up in Oregon. He'll be out of town a lot, so I'll have to get an emergency driver's license."

"No way," I said.

"Yep. I'll be legal to drive as soon as I pass the tests." Mike just beamed.

"Will they give you a license even though you're fourteen?" Favi asked. She went on without waiting for his answer. "I'll help you study for your written test."

"Can you drive us places?" I asked.

"I don't know. I have to get the license first."

We spent the rest of the ride talking about Mike's good luck. The bus pulled up to school before I'd said one word about my bull ride.

So I told them at lunch. "I went with Ben and Grandpa to the bull ring. And I rode a steer. It was a total rush. You wouldn't believe how it feels when they open the gate." I talked faster. "And after that, well I don't remember a lot, but it was even better than hitting a landing off that high ramp at the Winnemucca Skate Park. It's not like what I expected. It's awesome. I'm thinking about going back."

"You can't just decide to be a bull rider," Favi said, picking the tomatoes out of her sandwich. "That's not you."

"Sure he can, he just has to fall off about a thousand times." Mike ate one of Favi's tomatoes. "Then he'll learn how to stick on a bull—but it's not worth it."

"I can do it," I said to Favi. "Just like Mike can get his license."

"Well, I *need* that to drive my mom around. But bull riding—you don't have time," Mike said. "We're practicing for the skateboarding jam."

"I can do both."

"Just remember you said you'd skateboard *first*," Mike pressed. He reached for my chips. "Remember, we're boarders. That's what we do." He pushed his hair back off his forehead.

"Don't worry. He can't learn to bull ride that fast. Or maybe," Favi teased me the way she did when other kids might be listening, "they'll give you a real *nice* bull that anybody can ride."

I glared at her. "You can't score high on a nice bull."

"Maybe it would turn mean when you sit on it."

"Faviola, grow up," Mike said.

"Yeah, like you're the mature one." She stuffed her

garbage into her lunch bag. "I'd stick to skateboarding, Cam. Bull riding is too dangerous. It's almost *barbaric*." She used one of this week's vocabulary words. "You're a skater."

"I can do what I want, and that's what I'm gonna do." Now I sounded just like Ben. Or Grandpa.

"Well, if you are going to go off bull riding instead of practicing for the skate jam, don't be whining to me when you lose," Mike said. "You haven't landed a decent jump all week."

"I won't lose," I told him, and I smashed my lunch bag into the garbage.

My reputation was on the line. Bulls or no bulls, I had to prove to Mike that I could win the skateboard competition in Winnemucca.

When Lali and I came in from school, Grandma Jean had the kitchen full of cucumbers, green tomatoes, and onions from the garden. The whole place smelled like vinegar.

"Pickles!" Lali said. "Can I help?"

"Shhh, honey, Ben's sleeping." Grandma handed Lali the measuring spoons. "You can put in the peppercorns." Grandma turned to me and smiled. "Somebody around here mostly helps out by eating them. Cam, you can slice the cucumbers."

I knew how to do it. Grandma Jean made pickles every fall.

"What did you do today?" she asked. "Is that Mr. Killworth still as cranky as I remember?"

"Pretty much."

"You kids should loosen him up. Have you thought about filling his gym locker with shaving cream?"

"Grandma!"

"It's just an idea," she said. "Pretend I never said it."

We sliced and talked till the vegetables filled three big bowls. I helped Grandma Jean lift the heavy jars of pickles into a kettle of boiling water. Lali sang a song. "Pickles, pickles are green and red. Grandma's pickles are . . ." She couldn't find a rhyme. "Good," she finished. Suddenly, she looked serious.

"Grandma, can Ben eat the pickles? He can still eat pickles, can't he?"

"Of course he can." Grandma hugged her.

I realized that, for almost an hour, I hadn't thought about Ben. But I *was* thinking about what Mike said at lunch—that I was going to lose the skate jam. It was just a few days away, and I needed practice.

That night I convinced Mom that Killworth hadn't given us any homework. Of course, if she'd have been paying attention, she'd know that he gave us lots of homework every night, and that Monday was his favorite, because if you didn't get it done, then he had the whole week to bug you for it. But she was busy doing more accounting and more fretting about Ben, so she believed me about the homework and let me take my board out.

I headed for the Grange to board in the parking lot before it got dark. I used some stuff they had piled out back to set up a hurdle. Well, it was a piece of PVC pipe on two pieces of concrete. I ran up to it on my board, jumped the pipe in the middle of a kickflip, and landed like a pro. Then I raised the pipe higher for my next run. It wasn't like the real ramps and stuff we had at Mike's, but it would have to do. I was so into the jumps and kickflips that I didn't see Darrell walk up behind me, carrying a board.

"Looks good, kid," he said.

"I didn't know you had a board," I said.

"I told you I'd take you on—bull to board. I think I've got the edge on the bulls. So I'll give you a head start on the boards."

I laughed. "I don't need it. I'll take you. What can you do?"

Darrell looked around. "Let's get that jump higher and add some real turns."

He went to the field behind the Grange and came back carrying two big rocks. "Bring some more rocks over. We'll set up a course."

Darrell and I, we worked for a while. We used the rocks like slalom gates and set up two more hurdles. It was funny being there with Darrell. I hadn't seen him much since Ben had joined the service and Darrell'd taken a job selling ATVs and motorcycles down in Winnemucca. Of course, everyone knew he'd be at the bull ring any day there was practice, but until now, that wasn't exactly my spot to hang out.

"You should come by to see Ben," I said.

"Your brother and me, we *do* stuff. He don't want to sit around and talk to me," Darrell said.

"You don't know that." I balanced a PVC pipe to make another hurdle.

"You tell him hi for me. Right after I beat you." He

bopped me on the head. "Let's go. If I win, kid, I'm picking out a mean bull and you take another ride."

"And if I win, you do my algebra homework." I was counting on getting my homework done on time.

"I'll clock you." Being a bull rider, Darrell had a stopwatch button on his wristwatch. I ran my board around the course once to build up speed. Then I called to Darrell to start his watch and started between the first two rocks. I swung the board left and right under my feet. I could move it where I wanted by swaying my hips and knees, balancing over the wheels. I loved knowing exactly where I was going. I cut the corners as close as I could. I was flying and then I kicked off the board, landed my first jump, and moved between the next pair of rocks. I turned wide and had to slow down to make the next turn. I cleared another jump and was roaring to the last hurdle. It was the highest and when I jumped, I caught the pipe with my heel. I landed forward on my board and hit the asphalt hard with my shoulder. The pipe bounced along the asphalt with a hollow thunk.

"Too bad!" Darrell yelled.

I picked myself up. My shirt was torn and my shoulder was bleeding. "Crumb, I like this shirt," I said. "What's my time? You have to go faster."

"Nah, I just have to clear the last jump," he said.

"And go faster," I repeated.

Darrell pointed to the watch. "Don't worry. I'll do both." He tossed me the watch and started around the course. He had an easy balance that looked slow but he wove through the rocks like a dancer. Or a bull rider. He made the first jump and the second. The third jump came up just after a set of rocks. He kicked hard, jumped the pipe, landed on his board, turned ninety degrees, and skidded to a stop. "How'd I do?" he asked me.

"Well, you made the last jump, but you took an extra half a second."

"That's 'cause I finished," Darrell said, looking straight at me.

"But you didn't beat my time," I said.

"I didn't pass out, either." He slapped my back and laughed. "I think you owe me a bull ride."

"I think you should do my algebra," I said.

"Tell you what, squirt. You come to the bull ring tomorrow and bring your math. I'll help you out. Right after you ride."

I thought about Killworth and the extra problems he'd give the whole class if we didn't all get Monday's homework in by Wednesday. "Well, you didn't win," I said.

"And I didn't lose. See you at the bull ring." He took his board and walked toward his truck.

"I'm bringing my homework!" I yelled after him. He didn't look back.

✳ CHAPTER ✳

NINE

The thing was, since I rode the steer, I couldn't get bull riding out of my mind. I thought about it at strange times. Like, on the way to school when the bus passed the little herd we kept north of the road, I wondered if I could catch one of the steers and ride it. Mike interrupted my daydream.

"My mom got me all the papers to apply for my driver's license."

"Man, I want one," I said. "Do you have to take a driving test?"

"Yeah, but it shouldn't be hard."

It wouldn't be. Mike already knew how to drive. We all did, and we drove the trucks and tractors around on the ranches. But it would be cool to be street legal. Almost as cool as riding a bull.

That's what I mean. My thoughts always came back to bull riding. I wanted to feel the rush when the chute opened again. But it's hard doing something new in a small town. Everybody hears about what you are doing before you've hardly gone and done it. So it takes some guts to move past what everyone expects from you. Darrell's bet made it easy for me to try bull riding again, and on Tuesday, Grandpa gave me the excuse to go.

He came home from the grocery store beaming 'cause one of the old guys, Tom Lehi, I'm guessing, slapped him on the back and said he'd heard there was a new O'Mara bull rider coming up.

"What do you know?" Grandpa said. "They're already talking about your ride."

"You mean when I passed out."

Lali ran through and grabbed a box of crackers as Grandpa unloaded the grocery bag. "Don't let your Grandma Jean see that. It'll spoil your dinner." Lali giggled and kept going.

Grandpa turned to me. "That's just the first bull. Wait till you've ridden a few more. You'll learn fast."

I couldn't help smiling. "Can we practice now?"

"You sure?" he asked. "I don't want you to do nothing you don't have a heart for."

I didn't know if I had a heart for it. I was still bruised from my fall, but I had to try again, I knew that much. "Yeah, I want to."

"Hear that, Ben?" Grandpa said. "We've got ourselves another bull rider. Get your sorry butt out of bed and let's take him down to the arena and see how he goes this time."

Grandpa knew Ben couldn't get his butt out of bed, sorry or not, but it seemed the more Grandpa teased him, the more normal things were. We did the get-up, lift-into-the-chair thing and took off for the bull ring.

The closer we got, the more I fretted if I should do this. The skateboard competition was coming up in Winnemucca. I should be practicing 540s so I could beat Mike. But I'd gone and asked to ride now, so bull ring it was, one way or another.

There were fewer guys than before. Darrell was there and his dad, and a couple of cowboys who'd come down from McDermitt. As for bulls, it was Possum and the big Brahma, Quicksand, and a broken-down steer they called Rocket. Darrell came over soon as we drove up to help Ben into his chair. "The kid's gonna ride again, is he?"

"Gonna try," Ben said. "I figure he's in for a bull bashing." He laughed. It was a good day—easy to understand him. Darrell slapped Ben on the shoulder. How was it that Grandpa and Ben's friends could forget about Ben's head getting smashed and his arm blown clean off and act like they always had? I could forget for about a minute, but then I came right back to seeing him. Really seeing him—his sleeve tucked around the hook where his hand should be, and the stupid-looking blue helmet he wore everywhere but the bull ring. It was like the guy in the wheelchair wasn't exactly Ben but someone else who'd stepped in for a while.

Then Ben reached, as best he could with his right arm, under his jacket, pulled out his bull rope, and held it toward me. "Use this," he said.

My mouth dropped. Ben was superstitious about his gear. He never loaned his bull rope. But I took it and nodded at him. Darrell walked me over to the bucking chute. Three or four bulls were pacing around the ring. Their hooves crunched in the sand that padded the bottom of the arena. They snorted and one had drool coming out of his mouth. The bullfighter was a cowboy from out toward Unionville who came up sometimes just because he loved being in the ring with the bulls. He was good at it too. He whooped and whistled at the bulls and sent the bunch of them into the holding pen. Then Darrell loaded Rocket in the chute, dropped the bull rope, and motioned for me to hook it.

"So, how's Ben doing? Really?" Darrell asked me.

"He's okay. He doesn't say much about it."

"I wouldn't guess he'd complain," Darrell said. Then he added, "Bring your homework, squirt?"

I leaned across the chute to fish Ben's rope up. "Not so loud. Grandpa will kill me," I said.

"Like this steer isn't gonna?" Darrell smiled. "Catch the rope."

That was the easiest part of the bull ride. Hook the rope with the wire. Lali could even handle that once she found the darn thing. Darrell fixed the rope around Rocket and slapped him on his behind. The steer rammed the chute with his rump, shaking the whole contraption.

Standing on the platform, I took a moment to ponder the situation. Problem was, getting on a steer for the second time, I knew exactly what was coming—waiting for the gate to open, then the feeling like your stomach was dropping down through your feet. I swallowed hard. If Darrell, Ben, and Grandpa hadn't been watching, I wouldn't have gone over the side. I might have used the good sense that God gave me and climbed back down, but I didn't.

I tightened my knees so they wouldn't buckle, said a little prayer that I'd come out alive, and dropped onto Rocket. This time it was the steer that shivered under me, not the other way around. And soon as I touched him, the adrenaline started. I looked out at the arena. Grandpa had the gate, Darrell jumped down to bullfight, and the guys from McDermitt were on the fence, just in case. "Go to it, Cam!" one of them yelled. I put my hand through the handle, laid the rope into it, hit it closed to stick the pine tar, and then I whispered, "Go."

The gate came open and we jumped out. Rocket took a couple of steps and bucked up and down like a bronc, then rolled back on his hind legs. I wanted to catch myself with my free hand but stopped—that's not allowed. I leaned forward and pulled tight on the handle. For every move the steer made, my body did something on its own. It's not like I was meaning to do anything. I just rode. And then I fell off, hitting the dirt with my ankle and then my side. I rolled and crawled toward the fence, stood, and scrambled up the rails. Right then, the sun sparked off the grit in the arena like Fourth of July, and each breath I pulled in felt deeper than the last. I heard them yelling, "Way to go, Cam," and "That boy may stick on a bull yet." It was so fine. Then I felt the pain shooting up from my right foot.

Darrell rode and so did the McDermitt cowboys. Darrell went again, but I passed. I was thinking I was still alive and on a roll. And my ankle was swelling. As we left the ring, Darrell yelled after us, "Hey, Cam, call about that stuff I said I'd help with!"

"Cool," I answered. "I will."

— ✳ —

We got home about dinnertime. Ben was tired out, so Grandpa settled him in the living room. I went to the kitchen for some ice. "What's that for?" Mom asked.

"I'm just going to ice my foot."

"What happened? Did you fall off your board?"

Grandpa Roy came in just bursting with pride. He smiled like he had the best secret, but he couldn't hold it in. "No, Sherry, he landed on it coming off a steer. He's got guts."

My mom put down her spoon. She looked from me to Grandpa to Ben, who was already half-asleep. "Jim," she called to my dad, "did you hear that?" Her voice quivered.

"I did," Lali said. "Cammy fell off a steer."

"Uh-huh," Dad said. "I heard you were over at the bull ring. Next time, call me, Dad, and I'll come by."

This was so cool. Dad would come down from wherever to see me bull ride? He didn't give a whoop about my skateboarding.

"Jim!" Mom's voice pitched higher. "Bull riding!" Her face went red and her eyes filled up with tears. I couldn't tell if it was scared tears or mad ones, but they were coming fast. "I can't do it. We've got one son—" She stopped herself, thought, and then went on. "Look at you, Roy, you've lived with that bad hip for years. And Larry's got a plate in his head from being stepped on." She was talking about Larry Olson down toward Paradise. Everybody knew about how they had to put his skull back together after a bad throw. "Well, I can't stand it. Cam, you can't start bull riding. I've put up with it for years with this bunch and God knows how. But I'm not doing it, not anymore. I forbid it. I can't see both of my boys crippled."

Ben groaned. Grandpa Roy and Grandma Jean stared at her, and Lali looked like she was gonna cry. Dad said, "You didn't mean that, Sherry."

Mom shook her head and banged her hand on the counter. "I'm sorry, Ben," she whispered. Then she stared straight into my eyes. "But I meant what I said about you. Cam O'Mara, I won't lose another son. Not to war and not to bull riding. I'm your mother, and you stay away from that bull ring." She turned on Grandpa. "Make your own supper," she said, and stomped down the hall.

"She don't mean it," Grandpa Roy said to me.

"Yes, she does," Grandma Jean said. "If you don't know Sherry by now, you've been daydreaming all these years."

Grandpa looked blankly at the refrigerator.

"For heaven's sakes, I'll cook," Grandma Jean said.

My dad went down the hall after Mom.

For once it was Ben who was watching a fuss about me. I went over to him. "I'm sorry about what she said."

"Can't blame her," he said. "But . . . you better not ride . . . for a while."

I thought of how excited Ben was watching me and how I loved that part up on the chute where I didn't know if I'd ride or not. I loved the feeling that rose from my gut to my throat and expanded like the air itself was alive. Just then, there was only the bull and me and that expectation that shuddered through my whole body. I'd never felt anything like that. Not on a board, not on a horse. "We'll go back. Mom will get over it. She let you ride. She'll let me do it too."

"It's different," Dad said, coming up behind us.

"I don't get how it is," I said.

Dad sighed and shook his head. "Ben's bull riding . . .
That was before . . . No, she's serious right now. Mom's
fragile these days, and I'm with her on this. You can try
team roping if you want to do rodeo, but stay away from
the bull riding. She can't take it. Ben, no fault of yours," he
added. He handed me a fresh ice pack.

The ice helped my foot, though it swelled up some. To
tell you the truth, I was more ticked off about Mom than
about hurting my foot. Here I was, fourteen years old, and
she thought she could decide if I got on a steer or not. Well,
she didn't tell me not to board. I still had that.

✶ CHAPTER ✶

TEN

Saturday morning was the skateboard jam at the Winnemucca Skate Park. It was a Parks and Rec thing—the only competition around and most of the good boarders from Winnemucca to Battle Mountain and McDermitt to Austin would show up.

Grandpa and I made an early-morning run to drop some hay to the cattle in the high pasture. The feed was thin up there already. Then I fed the horses while Lali fed her goats. Mom had coffee going when we came in. She didn't say anything about last night. Neither did I. "We can all fit in Grandma Jean's Bronco on the way to Winnemucca since Grandpa's staying here with Ben."

"Ben's not going?" I asked.

"It's a long trip for him to go down there and back. We can't tire him out."

"But I might win," I said.

"Dad will take videos."

Videos weren't the same. "You can't just decide for him," I said.

Mom sighed. "There are more important things for Ben right now than going to your skateboard jam. He needs his strength. He'll see you another time."

"I went to his bull riding lots of times!"

"Cam, you know this is different."

"No, it's not."

I know I'm a jerk to say stuff like that about my brother, but just because he got shot up didn't change the way my family was. It just made me feel worse about saying it. And when we drove down to the Winnemucca Parks and Recreation Fall Skateboarding Jam, it was Grandpa and Ben, the two people I wanted there the most, who stayed behind. And that wasn't the end of it.

First it snowed. Yeah, it was hot in September, and now it was snowing in October, but weather's changeable, and the wind blew in from the north. I met Mike and waved at his folks. We signed in and got our numbers in a snow flurry. Snow doesn't bother me when we're dropping hay to the cattle, but it's tricky when you're on a skateboard.

The Winnemucca Skate Park is on the edge of a city park, right by the road. You can look across the lawns and see train tracks and then the mountains. It's a pool-shaped deal. You'd think a small town like that would have one of those little flat parking-lot skate parks that the Boy Scouts build, with a chain-link fence and a couple of ramps and a rail, but this is a full-on hole dug into the ground with rounded sides, ramps, and concrete benches built into the side. It's got lights for night skating, too, and there's a playground with a bouncy purple dinosaur right there. Lali took off to ride on it the minute she jumped out of the Bronco, with Grandma Jean trotting right behind her.

The Parks and Rec guy went inside and came out with a push broom and got one of the kids busy sweeping snow off the ramps. It piled into the pockets at the bottom of the pool, and he shoveled it into a plastic bucket.

"You think it's going to ice up?" I asked Mike.

"Naw, the sun's coming out. It'll melt."

"I'd rather skate when it's dry," I said. I checked the underside of my skateboard, the trucks and wheels, to make sure everything was all working right.

Mike grinned. "It doesn't matter if it's wet. Just as long as you're ready to come in second."

"Shut up," I said. "You can't jump that board over a garden hose."

He poked my back with his board. "I'm gonna win, you know."

"Shut up," I said again. I popped a couple of aspirins I got from Grandma Jean's purse. My bruised foot throbbed against my tennis shoe. "Check out the rest of these guys."

There were some boarders in the lineup we knew from practicing in Winnemucca. They were older, and they usually ignored us or offered us cigarettes and laughed when we wouldn't take 'em.

"Hey, Cam, you trying for the big-time here?" one guy asked. "Did you bring your mama along?"

I didn't pay him any mind. He was a senior, and he always gave me a hard time because I was better than him—and had been since I was about twelve.

His friend chimed in. "At least his mama wants to see him skate. Yours won't watch 'cause she don't want to see you get wiped up by a couple of ninth graders."

"Ninth graders?" one of the guys from Battle Mountain said. "Man, I thought that one was our age." He pointed to me. Then he started practicing some tricks. The three boarders from Battle Mountain were good. Could be Mike and me would both come in second to them anyway.

Mike was up first. It was kind of a freestyle competition that a couple of guys who worked at the park cooked up. They'd made this routine that took you down into the bottom of the pool, up one side, and down again. We had to use a couple of the ramps, land a jump—any kind—and do a 50-50, and then go back around to the beginning. After that, you could let go and do what you wanted till three more minutes were up. But no flips. Even if somebody could land one, the park didn't want the liability.

They lined up three judges at a card table. They were older guys who were done with high school but still hung out at the skate park when they weren't working. They scored your tricks—how hard they were and how good you did them. That worked for me. I could always catch a lot of air.

Mike started off. I hoped the combination of the snow and the audience would rattle him, but no such luck. He flew down the ramps and around the turns. Mike was good at skating vert up the sides of the pool. When he was at the top, he did a rock and roll with a 180 kickturn, which flipped him and his board around to take him back into the bowl. Once he looked like he was going to lose his board, but I knew better. Mike could look out of control, but he wasn't. He landed square and kept running. Everyone went nuts yelling. He coasted to a stop at the top of the pool, turned, and waved like he was royalty or something.

Next the boys from Battle Mountain took their shots. Anybody could see that they weren't going to catch Mike on difficulty, so it was my turn to win it—or not. I got through the "compulsories" as they called it and on to my part. I ran down into the hole, up again, turned onto the first ramp, shot across with my board right under my feet, and landed low and solid. Someone called out, "Bustin!" I used the speed to get me up on a curb and I 50-50ed along it. Next, I did a 360, turned 180, and was flying along, feeling great. I went to a 5-0 to set up my next shot into the pool, and then my ankle just folded. It slammed down on me like the school bus stop sign. I smashed into the concrete, tumbled down the side of the pool, and landed in the puddle of melting snow. My board went sailing and so did my chances. I lay there for a minute and then popped to my feet. I'd torn a hole clean through my jeans, and my right side was scraped raw from my waist to my armpit.

Mike won. His mom took a bunch of pictures and the Parks and Rec gave him a tricked-out new skateboard and a certificate to a boarding shop.

"Nice board," I said.

"You should have practiced more," Mike said.

"I practiced. I busted my ankle, that's all."

"Busted your ankle riding a stupid bull," Mike said.

"It didn't hurt you none," I said. "I'd have won if I didn't mess up my ankle."

"Yeah, and I'd have lost—is that what you're saying? Except, gee, I didn't spend my weekend bull riding and ignoring my real friends." Mike walked off.

I spit on the new snow. I'd lost. I was glad Darrell wasn't there to rub it in too. And more, I was glad Ben had stayed home.

Mom put her arm around me as we walked to the car. Her hand stung my bruised shoulder.

"You hurt that ankle worse than we thought. Do you think you need an X-ray?" She was really asking herself. But I answered.

"I'll be okay. I can get it from here." I brushed her arm aside and limped faster, moving ahead of her.

"You'll do better next time," she said. "You will." She waited for me to agree with her. But a train barreled by. It made plenty of noise and I didn't have to answer.

If it wasn't already my worst day, it took the prize when we stopped by the post office on the way home. Report cards were in our PO box. I opened the envelope while we were driving. Mom reached over and took the printout almost before I could finish reading. "What do you mean getting a C in history? And a C+ in algebra?" Mom demanded. "I'll have to talk to Mr. Killworth about that. Honestly, Cam, I can't believe you let your grades go. And don't even think about saying you didn't have time to study. You found time for skateboarding and sneaking off to bull ride."

"I didn't sneak off, Grandpa took me. And my grades aren't bad. That stuff is hard."

"It's never been hard before. And you should know to do your part without asking, especially now, with Ben home. We don't have time for this." She stopped talking, like she had to think on just how mad she could get. "Okay, you can just hand over that skateboard. I'm keeping it. It's chores and homework for you until your next report card."

"Till my next report card? That's six weeks. My muscles will shrivel up. I'll forget how to jump."

Dad pulled the Bronco to the side of the road, turned, and leaned against the door, just looking at me. "Stop with the whining, Cam. And watch what you say. Ben has real problems with his muscles, you know. It's not something you should be joking about."

I wasn't joking. You have to keep boarding. It's natural, like bull riding. I can't explain how my legs know how to kickflip or how my butt stays on top of a bull, but it works if you just keep doing it.

"Just don't blame me for stuff I didn't do," I said. "I don't sneak."

"He's right," Grandma Jean said. "Cam wouldn't do anything sneaky."

"This is between Cam and Jim and me," my mother said. Her voice was flat and cool, like she was holding herself together with just words.

Dad drove the rest of the way home and pulled into the driveway. I jumped out and went around back toward the barn. No skateboarding, no bull riding. Mike was mad at me for slacking off on our boarding practice, and Mom, she was the one who hadn't even asked me about my homework since Ben got hurt. She just doctored him and took on more ranch accounts for other people. Well, I could get as worked up as her. I picked up the axe by the woodpile, lined up three rounds of pine and whaled into one. The ax sunk deep, then kicked back against my shoulders. I swung again, harder, and the wood split clean through with a *crack*. I sucked in the pine smell and hammered it again. Splitting kindling is just the thing to do when you really want to bust your hand through a wall but know better.

That Monday, Killworth chewed me out too. He'd talked to Mom.

"O'Mara, your algebra is weak, and you are behind in your history assignments. I'm relieving you of PE. You can use the time to get your history turned in. As for algebra, you should get a tutor. If your grades don't come up, we'll add some after-school sessions for you. Am I clear?"

"Yes, sir." I didn't want to tick him off and have to clean the whole school or run laps on the track or something. Killworth loved laps. He said it wasn't punishment because he ran them with you. He called it a "health opportunity" or "attitude adjustment."

"You're not like half these other fools, O'Mara. Get yourself together. I'm expecting you to make the right decisions here."

This was sabotage. Between my mother and Killworth, they'd have me learning to knit with Grandma Jean or playing hopscotch with Lali. And an algebra tutor? Mom and Dad were still paying off the airline tickets and motels bills from when they'd gone to DC to be with Ben.

There was no way I could ask them to pay for a tutor.

When I came in from school, I stopped at Favi's. If I couldn't board with Mike, I could play video games with her. But she wasn't home. Figured.

I headed home and, as I came in the door, Grandma Jean called, "Is that you, Cam? Come up to my room."

I went in and she patted the bed for me to sit next to her.

"Things aren't going so well for you, Cam," she said. "So I made this for you." She pressed a navy blue plastic packet into my hand. "It's like mine. I think you need an angel now."

"Grandma, I don't think angels worry about me."

"There's salt from the Salt Lick in there too," she said.

I opened the little snap at the top and peeked inside. There were bits of sage and the salt and a little silver heart. I could see a St. Jude medal, and there was other stuff I couldn't name.

Grandma Jean took the bag and closed it. "No matter what's *in* there. It's special for you and nobody else's business. Don't show it off. But keep it with you. It will help."

I didn't think it would help at all, but I pushed the little bag down into my jeans pocket.

"That's a good boy," she said, and she kissed my head.

ELEVEN

Mom took my skateboard and went right back to life as usual.

On Wednesday she drove Ben to the VA hospital in Reno for an assessment. When I came in from school, Mom and Ben were already home. The look on Ben's face told me something was up. "Hey, bro', guess what?" he said. "I can feel a pinprick in my ankle. That's good. Like a miracle."

"So what'd the doctors say?"

"They say if I work hard, I might walk."

"Wow." I whistled. This was a miracle, for sure. "So what do you have to do? How long till you can walk?"

"Don't know. But I will. You bet on it."

Going from feeling a prick on your ankle to walking— that would be a real trick. But that was way too mean to say, so instead I answered, "I'll be waiting on that."

And when you stop your own thoughts from coming out of your mouth, don't you wonder what other folks are doing with theirs? What else was inside Ben's head that he wasn't saying? Was he mad that I had my legs and could do stuff like skateboarding, even if I was grounded? Was he mad that he had to go back to California so he could learn to twitch his toes? He was hoping for so *little* of what the rest of us still had. Honestly, his excitement made me kind of sad.

I tried to cheer myself up. "It can't be tougher than getting thrown from a bull or hiking Wheeler Peak the time we got caught in a whiteout. Remember that?"

Ben looked at me blankly. "I don't remember Wheeler Peak. Some stuff is gone."

How could he forget that? We'd done it in June just before he left. "You don't remember Wheeler Peak?" I said. "What about the high school championship rodeo?"

"I remember that," he said. Then Ben smiled.

"They'll work on your memory in Palo Alto too," Mom said.

Well, if Ben was excited, Mom was feeling down. She had been content having Ben under her roof and knowing he was safe, even if he wasn't quite whole. But she had to see, like the rest of us did, that the idea of therapy, of standing up again, made him more whole of a person than he'd been since he'd come home. So, even though he had three days left of his leave, she and Dad loaded Ben into the pickup and headed west to California. They took Ben back to the TBI unit and spent the weekend in Palo Alto.

I took it as my chance to get a little elbow room. Saturday morning, I helped Grandpa Roy change the oil in the tractor.

Then, I took one of the cow horses, Pepper, out for a ride. I started out like I was going over to the Jones's ranch but turned the horse around once we were on the main road, and rode to the bull ring. Mom hadn't told me I couldn't watch, and Darrell Wallace was my best bet for getting help with algebra.

"Hey, squirt, are you going to ride again?" Darrell asked.

"Naw, I just came to watch."

"Too much for you?"

"Too much for my mom. She went nuts when she found out I'd been riding."

Darrell scratched his head. "So, I don't see her here now."

I tied Pepper to a little cottonwood tree and climbed the fence to look at the weekend's bulls. Trucks were coming down the road and rumbling onto the gravel. When they filled that area, they parked on the road.

"What's going on?" I asked.

"We're having a kind of fall jubilee. A bunch of us decided to meet and see who could go the most rounds on those bulls. There's a jackpot—fifty dollars each. If you ante up and win, the money's yours—split for first, second, and third."

"My mom won't let me ride and I don't have fifty dollars," I said.

There were about ten bulls and big steers milling around in the holding pen. One of them was the black Brahma, Quicksand. "So who draws the big one?" I asked. "He's a piece of work."

Darrell spit. "Naw, he ain't nothing compared to Ugly. That bull makes 'em all look puny. And that's the one I'm going to ride someday. Ugly. You know they have a purse on him. The outfit that raises the bucking bulls wants some exposure, and they've put up a prize that'd make a pig dance. They're paying fifteen thousand dollars to the first cowboy to ride him. That's gonna be me."

"Could be me." I grinned.

"Yeah, but your momma won't let you. And by the time you're old enough to sign all the papers for the insurance waivers yourself, I'll have gone and rode him. You'll have to wait for the next crazy big bull to come along."

Actually, that suited me fine. Right now, sitting on the fence, I was longing for the adrenaline rush, but I didn't long to die. The big bulls scared me, and I could get my fix off a smaller steer any day. But I'd come for something else.

"Darrell, I'm about to crash and burn in algebra, and if I don't work it out, my folks are going to have a heart attack. So, I'm thinking, can you help me with my homework now?"

"I'm about to ride some bulls, kid, but stick around, and we'll take a look after the event."

So that's how I came to ignore my mom and get on a bull again. I didn't mean to. Really. But the cowboys just kept lining up and one after the other, they lowered themselves into the bucking chute. Most of the guys recognized me.

"Aren't you Ben O'Mara's kid brother? You gonna take a round?"

Well, I did say no a few times, but then one of them offered to waive the jackpot money and let me ride for practice. Temptation got the best of me. Mom or not, I borrowed a bull rope and rigged up a little spotted bull. I was nervous without Ben and Grandpa there. But Darrell took the gate duty and gave me a wink as I slipped onto the bull. I remembered Grandpa shouting to square my shoulders and then I called out, "Go."

Darrell pulled the gate, and me and that bull took a ride. This time felt different. I relaxed over his shoulders and let him make the moves. I gripped with my left hand and he spun right, giving me some good pull against the handle. Every time he hit the ground, I was still there, getting ready for the next jolt. I could hear the guys screaming, and then Darrell kept yelling, "Time, time, you're done!"

Eight seconds. I'd made it. I ripped the tail of the bull rope—it was squeezed tight between the rope handle and my fingers, glued down by the pine tar on my glove. When I pulled, it unzipped right through my fingers, and with that, I caught some air—flying high off to the side of the bull. I landed easy, though the jarring hurt my ankle, and I ran for the fence.

"Great ride, kid!"

"Eight seconds. The kid moves to the next round."

And I got to the third round, too. Darrell called it O'Mara magic or beginner's luck. I'm thinking it was more the luck, or maybe it was lazy bulls? Whatever it was, I was happy to take it. There were only three of us in the third round. Me, Darrell, and a big guy, who I thought was Favi Ruiz's uncle from Lovelock. No one else had made two eight-second rides. Andrew wrote out the bulls' names so we could draw, official like, for the next ride. Darrell reached into Andrew's hat and pulled the spotted bull I'd ridden in the first round. Favi's uncle drew an albino Brahma, and I got Quicksand. Next to him, his buddy Possum was a pussy cat. My stomach flipped and growled. My rides had gone too well for my own good, and now I was stuck getting on the biggest bull there.

"Quicksand," Andrew said again. "Cam, do you want another draw? He's just started riding," Andrew explained to the cowboys.

I knew what I had to answer. "I'll take what I get." But when my turn came, Darrell had to step on the Brahma's back to rig the bull rope, his body was so broad.

"This here's the bull I'll practice on for Ugly," Darrell said.

"And it's the bull I'm going to ride today," I said. I wished I believed it.

I jumped around to get my adrenaline going, and then, when I got to the chute, I closed my eyes and tried not to look. I was shaking again. I blocked out the cowboys yelling for me. I needed all my faculties to stay on this bull. They sprung the gate, I opened my eyes just long enough to see his black ears and golden eyes about as big as marbles, and then I whizzed right over his head and hit the dust.

I brushed myself off and headed toward the fence.

"Too bad, Cam," Andrew said, patting my back. "That's a lot of bull for a beginner."

As I walked away, Darrell jogged up behind me.

"Good ride," he said. "Listen, did you bring your algebra?"

"Yeah, it's here." I pulled the assignment out of my back

pocket, unfolded it, smoothing out the creased squares.

We sat on the tailgate of his truck and did a couple of problems together. When we finished, he said, "E-mail me if you have trouble and I'll help you online."

"Thanks, man."

"Listen, does Ben have e-mail in Palo Alto?"

"Yeah, he gets online when he can."

"Cool, I think I'll check in with him," Darrell said. "You know, he sure was fun to compete with. I wish . . . " He didn't finish. Darrell put his hands in his pockets and said, "I almost forgot. This fell out when you were riding." He held out the little blue bag Grandma Jean had made. "What is it?"

"Just stuff from my grandma. I forgot to put it away." I shoved it down into my jeans.

Darrell backed out in his truck and I pulled myself onto Pepper to ride home. I turned the horse onto the road and fingered the packet from Grandma Jean. I couldn't help wondering if she was right. I shouldn't have stuck on two bulls. Not yet. What if it really was the salt?

✷ CHAPTER ✷

TWELVE

My folks came back from Palo Alto on Sunday night. They'd hardly been home for an hour when Mom announced, "Cam, we're going over to see Ben next weekend. You and Lali can come too."

"I can stay here with Grandpa if you need me to," I said. It would be another chance to ride the bulls, and hospitals gave me the creeps.

"Grandpa's coming too. So's Grandma Jean. We're all going."

I looked to Dad for a little help, but he had his nose in the newspaper. "What about the stock?" I asked. "Mike could come over. His dad's helping him practice for his driver's test this weekend, but when he's done he can sleep over and we could watch the stock."

"You're not quite ready for that, buddy," Dad said, looking over his reading glasses. "I'll ask Ruiz to do it." Now, Grandpa's stubborn, but Dad's orderly. Heck, he named us in alphabetical order, well, almost. My cousin Adam Carl, the one who drowned, he took up the A's in Dad's mind, so he started with Ben, then me, then Lali, who's named Dalia for real. Dad has his own way of doing everything, and Oscar Ruiz would do it just the way Dad liked. There was no use arguing to stay home.

I'd been thinking Palo Alto was far enough away that I wouldn't have to see Ben in a real hospital. At home, I'd gotten used to his routine, and if I was uncomfortable, well, I could offer to dry dishes or go clean some stalls. But now they were going to take me to him in the hospital—to his medication smells and his blasted-off arm. The stump was as hard to think about as the drawn-out words and useless leg. And there was the scar that hid up there by his neck. I hadn't seen it much, except where it peeked out of his collar. He was careful to keep his shirt buttoned up. I had no idea what Ben looked like now in those places where the explosion hit him. Would that stuff all show if he was in a hospital gown? And what about the other guys in the hospital? What if they were really bad off too? I didn't want to see some guy with burned off ears or no legs. I didn't want to think about the explosions and the war. I plain didn't want to go.

I spent the week doing history and algebra and trying not to be cranky with Mom. My feet just itched to skateboard, and I couldn't get away from wanting a try at Quicksand again. Mom was keeping track of me since I was grounded. But she did let me out on Wednesday afternoon to go over to Mike's.

"We have a speech to practice for English," I said.

"Can't he come here?"

"His mom is painting their dining room and she wants him there in case she needs something. And who knows, she might faint again."

"She's always redoing that house, isn't she? You'd think she'd slow down a little now." Mom thought for a moment and then she let me go, saying, "Be home by five thirty."

I rode my bike to Mike's and leaned it against his porch. He met me before I got up the stairs. "Want to try my new skateboard?"

I didn't want to ride *that* skateboard. He'd won it at the Winnemucca Jam. But I wanted to ride. "I'll use your old one," I said.

Mrs. Gianni really was painting her dining room, and she certainly wasn't thinking about my mom grounding me. So we pulled out the ramps and coasted around the driveway on Mike's boards. The wheels vibrated under my feet and sent familiar feelings up my legs. I pumped fast and leaned into the board. I ollied off the ramp, turning in the air, and just kept skating. My ankle didn't hurt anymore.

"This is awesome," I said.

"You know it," Mike answered. "Boarding isn't so fun without you."

"Boarding isn't any fun at all when my mom's got my skateboard," I said.

"Can't you get it back?" Mike did a 360 and slid past.

"You know my mom. I was lucky to talk her into this. She's all over me about my homework."

Five o'clock came too fast. I left Mike with two boards under his arm and biked home. It was the only boarding I did all week. Instead, I was memorizing dates and factoring polynomials.

I was e-mailing Darrell my algebra problems to check when Lali tapped me on the shoulder. "Cammy, stop studying and come see Pretty. She's a circus goat!" I followed Lali outside to the goat pen. Lali had painted big polka dots on Pretty with grape-drink mix she'd swiped from Grandma Jean's bag and then she'd tied a tutu around the goat's neck. No one could get peeved with Lali when she did stuff like that. I would have been grounded for an extra week.

"Lali, where ever did you get the idea to do that?" Mom asked, and she took pictures of Lali and Pretty. I stopped working on the algebra and filled up the wading pool with water. We tossed in a beach ball and Grandma Jean tried to get the goat to kick it out. Pretty ended up biting it, and the whole thing deflated like an old balloon.

"We'll have to work on that trick, Lali," Grandma Jean said.

"And Cam has to work on his homework," Mom reminded me. What was wrong with this picture?

Finally, the week and the studying were over. Saturday morning I threw my duffel bag in the back of the pickup and I rode with Grandpa. Dad, Mom, Grandma Jean, and Lali took the Jeep. We left before sunrise, which is ear-freezing cold in mid-November, and drove straight through to Reno. Of course, Lali had to stop to pee every couple of hours, and Grandpa Roy didn't seem to mind getting out to stretch either, so we stopped at Donner Pass, and Lali and I made snowballs with our bare hands and threw them at each other. Then we smashed some up against the pine trees until our fingers turned red and stinging.

"I'm cold, Cammy. And I'm hungry."

"That's because we're at Donner Pass. This is where a bunch of pioneers in a wagon train got stuck in the snow. They were stranded here for months and then they *ate* each other," I growled at her.

"No, they didn't." She stomped her foot and crossed her arms. "You're teasing me."

"I am not. Ask your teacher," I said. "But let's get you in the Jeep to get warm. Mom has snacks, too." I carried her to the car and belted her in.

We drove down the mountain and stopped again at Gold Run before we left the forest, then took a long haul into Sacramento. The air got damp as we dropped into the Central Valley, and winter haze hung over the fields. We drove through for fast food that we ate in the car and got to the edge of the Bay Area after lunch.

I'd been there a couple of times before, when Mom got it in her head we should go to an art museum or see the Golden Gate Bridge, but that was when I was little and before Lali was even born. Now, the concrete cramped in around me, suffocated me with cars and buildings. It smelled like oil, and there was a dull roar from all those city people doing what they do. It's a sound you don't hear on the desert. Grandpa didn't seem to mind, except for swearing at the drivers and wondering why half of them weren't dead already from the way they shot in and out of the lanes. My hands were sweaty from gripping the door handle, and I was praying I wouldn't be dead that very afternoon. I'd never seen so many cars on one piece of highway.

We got to Palo Alto before dinner. The Marines put us up in a motel, but there was a mix-up and we had one room for all of us. Mom and Dad and Grandma Jean set down their suitcases, claiming the two beds. It looked like Grandpa Roy would get the sofa.

"Where do I sleep?" Lali asked.

"I'll find some blankets for you and Cam," Mom said.

Great. After all this, Lali and I would sleep on the floor.

Mom kept talking. "I can't wait to see Ben. To see how he's doing."

I wished I could say the same, and I wished I weren't grounded from skating and had brought my board. The one thing this place had going for it—there was a lot of concrete. But board or not, the motel had a pool, and Lali and I promised each other that it didn't matter if it was November, we'd swim that evening.

We all squeezed into the Jeep for the ride to the VA hospital. Lali wore a dress and kept fussing about getting it wrinkled.

"Ben won't care about your dress," I said.

"He will. I want him to see it. It has daisies," she said, pointing to its big yellow flowers.

"He'll see those," I said. "For sure."

Just then a siren went off behind us, and Lali about jumped in my lap. "It's okay." I hugged her up to me. "That's just city stuff." But in my head, I was wondering how all these people stood being so packed up together. I wondered if Ben could feel it too from inside the hospital.

The VA hospital was huge. And brick. It stretched out from the parking lot like the university in Reno. I bet the whole town of Salt Lick could live on just one floor of that place. Families and all kinds of vets made a steady stream through the revolving doors, while more waited by the curb for buses and vans that zipped around like bees. As Dad parked the Jeep, my heart started racing. I wanted to see Ben. We went into a smaller building off to the side that was for guys with traumatic brain injury. There were a couple dozen of them, and with the war and all, every bed was full. The halls echoed, and when we passed a room, you'd hear just a clip of what the guys were saying. This one had a Texas drawl, and that one was on the phone with someone back home in Colorado. Some were sitting with family, and there was a nervousness from those rooms that you could feel.

I peeked in the door as we passed. The patients who I could see were all messed up like Ben, and instead of that making me feel better, like he had company, my throat tightened up. What had happened to them all? Did those improvised explosive devices, the IEDs, send shock waves through all their brains? Who knew these guys were all here? Did anybody say, "Thank you, we know you got blown to pieces, so sorry, and now just put your life back together?" Did anyone say, "Gee, we hope this was worth your leg or your arm or half your face?" We turned another corner and Mom about flew into Ben's room. The whole bunch of us squeezed in as best we could. Ben was sitting in his wheelchair and reached out with his good arm to hug her.

"Did you miss us, honey?" she asked.

"'Course," he answered.

Dad took a chair next to Ben's wheelchair, and Lali and I stood at the end of his empty bed.

"You can sit," Ben said. "How's bull riding, bro'?"

"I'm not doing that," I lied. It was hard talking about bulls in this place. It made me wish Ben was home with us in our living room.

"Ask me about Pretty," Lali said.

"What about her, Lollipop?" Lali only let Ben call her that.

"I made her a circus goat." Then Lali told him all about dressing up Pretty.

When Lali was done, Mom asked, "How's the therapy going?"

"Okay," Ben said.

"Really? How is it?"

Ben looked at his lap, then at her, and back at his one hand. He sighed. "I get tired."

Mom took his hand and I backed up till I about touched Grandpa in the doorway.

"So," Mom went on, like no one was there but her, "I thought maybe Cam and Grandpa could stay and keep you company while Dad and I do some paperwork with the hospital. They have a lot of forms we can help you with."

"Lali and I will be a pair," Grandma Jean said. She pulled a deck of cards out of her bag. "Crazy Eights?" she said, and dealt two hands.

Well, that was it. I was trapped in this freak place. Grandma Jean acted like she owned it, Mom and Dad were preoccupied with all the hospital stuff to do with Ben, and Grandpa Roy was standing mute in the doorway. I'd take off, but I didn't know how to walk back to the motel, and

I'd probably get flattened by a cement truck or end up in a junkyard with crazy dogs jumping at me. Why did Ben have to be *here*?

"So, bro', push me. I'll give you a tour."

"Can you leave your room?" I asked.

"I do it every day," he said, smiling.

"Grandpa can take you," I said.

"I'm going to sit down right here and supervise this card game. Your grandmother cheats," Grandpa said, pulling over a chair.

That didn't leave me much choice. I kicked the brake off of Ben's wheelchair and took the handles. The wheels spun easy against the vinyl floor. I pushed him into the hallway. I had an urge to run down the hall and let him go, to see how far the chair would glide. But I didn't do it. Instead I walked, each step echoing through the corridor.

"Turn here," Ben said. I turned right, and at the end of a short hallway, we came to a big room. A few men sat around, playing checkers with their families or watching TV. One guy called out to Ben.

"So, is this your little brother you keep talking about?"

I didn't want to stare, but this guy's face was burned and half his hair was gone. So were his legs. Was it ruder to turn away or just to look? I figured I'd look. He had bigger problems than who looked at him.

"Yeah, this is Cam." Ben was talking better today. "You know, my buddies say he's something on a bull. They say he's gonna be one of Nevada's best."

My jaw dropped. What buddies? Did Darrell tell him I was riding again?

"Good thing he lives in Nevada," the burned man said. "We've got some hot riders back home in Georgia. I'm Matt Burton," he said, holding out his hand.

I shook it and looked at him straight on. "You bull ride?"

"No, I'm not that stupid. But I know a few, and Georgia will take on Nevada any day for crazy men doing stunts. Right, Ben?" He turned to me. "Ben and I were in the same unit, though you wouldn't recognize me from the pictures now, would you?" He laughed, but I couldn't let myself do that. I kept staring.

"We had some good times on the base. Remember when Gonzales tried to eat ten hamburgers in two minutes at the McDonald's?"

Ben laughed. "He threw up."

"Everywhere, man. Tables, floor. It was gross. Or how about when Jacobs went to run in the morning and you'd stuck the bottoms of his shorts together with superglue? He jumped into those and fell right on his can. We did some crazy stuff." The marine shook his head and laughed.

"Listen, Cam," Burton went on, "your brother won't tell you, so I will. I wouldn't be alive at all if Ben hadn't put a tourniquet on my leg and held me together while the medevac copter came in. I'd have bled to death. It's ironic we're both here now, don't you think?"

"Wow, Ben, that's neat."

Ben shrugged. "I don't exactly remember."

I knew Ben couldn't remember stuff, but this was big. He didn't remember saving this guy's life?

"Was that when you got hit? When you were helping him?" I asked.

Ben looked blank. "I don't think so."

"No, it was different. Your brother and I were sweeping through houses looking for insurgents in this nasty neighborhood. Even the kids there would have killed us if they got the chance. Most everyone was gone, and we were bashing through the doors, to be sure the area was clean. Somebody'd left a booby trap, though, and I was the one who found it." He nodded to his legs. "It blew me clear out of the room. I remember it all. Most days I wish I couldn't.

"It didn't matter that I was smashed on the ground. They just kept firing all around. The noise makes a rhythm that gets in your head. You just keep hearing it, *rat-a-tat-tat*," he drummed his fingers as he said it, "and you know each shot could kill you. Well, Ben came in right behind me and tore the sleeves off his shirt to tie up my legs."

"I remember the blood," Ben said, "that's all."

"I left a lot of me on that courtyard in Baghdad." Burton stopped and took a swig from a water bottle.

"But they didn't get all of me. Your brother stayed there and lay on my belly, holding the blood in my legs until the medevac came in. They shot me up with something for the pain, and then I don't remember. But I know I would be gone on to the next world if it weren't for Ben. And now, here we both are. Good enough, still in the same outfit."

He looked at Ben. "You got hit a couple weeks later."

"It was morning," Ben said. "I remember getting my gear on and loading into a truck. We weren't going far." He stopped.

"Did you save some people that day, too?" I asked. "Or did you get hit first?"

"I don't remember," he said. "I just remember the sound and the smell—like rotten eggs and burning oil. Burning hair. Foul. That smell was enough to make you puke. That's it."

"You pass out," Georgia said. "A lot of the guys pass out and don't remember."

They both got real quiet. I didn't know what else to say, so I changed the subject. "So, did Darrell talk to you? You know I've been bull riding?"

"Uh-huh."

"You can't tell Mom," I said, quietly, "but I rode Quicksand."

"They put you on Quicksand?" Ben's eyes lit up.

Georgia cocked his head and pointed his finger my way. "So is that bull as bad as his name?"

"He's big. Real big. I didn't make a time."

"But Darrell said you rode twice, eight seconds, right?" Ben asked me.

"True." I blushed.

"That's good, Cam," Ben said. "That's a plain miracle for a new rider. Just go again. You'll stick on Quicksand."

Georgia laughed. "That's the way, ain't it? You get knocked down and you just go again. Bull riders and jarheads. That's the way."

There was a long silence. I looked around the room and took it in. The sun poured through the windows lighting bright squares on the floor. The walls had posters with upbeat sayings like, "If life gives you lemons, make lemonade." It was enough to make you gag. What lemonade? Ben wasn't the youngest one here. Geez, a lot of them could pass for my age. There were some older guys, maybe twenty-eight or thirty, who were broken up pretty good too. The war seemed to be an equal-opportunity destroyer. The casualties, as the service called them, came in every color and size. What these guys had in common was the wheelchairs and walkers. The helmets and slippers. Missing body parts and scars.

"When I'm done here, I'm going back to Iraq to kick some butt," Georgia said.

"You and me too," Ben said.

My heart skipped. I didn't hear that right. "You'd go again?" My voice cracked. "But why?"

"Our buddies are there," Ben said. "We got their back."

THIRTEEN

I was glad to leave. I couldn't say so to my family, but after seeing those guys, you stew about stuff. Things like, what was worth losing a year of your life, half your arm, and half your memories? Ben said he wanted to go back to Iraq, but okay, would a sane person do that? Was he working on half his cylinders? The military folks talked about fallen heroes, but what I saw was guys like Ben and me. Was it me with the screw loose? Was I unpatriotic?

Dad took the truck and left early. The rest of us drove home with a pile of paperwork from the VA and a new teddy bear for Lali. I hated leaving Ben there. Mom felt the same. "I can't stand that he's alone there. You know, I just wish there was more family around. If Uncle Harlan hadn't died, he could visit. He lived in Hayward."

"Lord, that would be worse than more of it," Grandma Jean said. "Uncle Harlan would bore him to death and then Ben'd leave this earth with bad jokes ringing in his ears.

Now, I loved my brother, but I don't wish his corny jokes on anyone."

"Seems that don't matter, since he's already dead," Grandpa Roy said.

"Will you stop talking about dead people?" Mom said. "I just meant Ben's alone here, and Salt Lick is so far away."

She got that right. Salt Lick was nine hours, if there wasn't snow, and about a light-year, if you considered how different the ranch and the hospital felt. I put my baseball cap on and pulled it over my eyes so I could sleep.

"There's always a bright side, look for that," Grandma Jean said. "We all have our angels."

I tried to imagine good stuff. I thought of Ben standing up, dressed for bull riding in his hat, jeans, and boots. I thought of him walking. The car hummed along the highway and I fell asleep.

It was dark when we got home. Grandpa Roy went right out to help Oscar Ruiz with the evening chores, and Grandma Jean started dinner. Dad and Mom sat down with the papers from the hospital, their bills, and the bank statement.

"I'm not borrowing anything," Dad said. "I've got the loan on this year's alfalfa and the Angus stock to pay off. You know we can't borrow more."

"Well, we could go to social services and see if there's some relief for us, somehow," Mom said.

Dad just stared at her. "We're falling short, that's all. Since you lost your job, we've got to make up the income. We'll handle it."

"How?" Mom asked.

"We can still tighten our belts. That's the good news."

Dad's idea of good news was a piece different from mine.

"I could pawn the silver," Mom said.

"But I like the pretty silver," Lali piped in.

"We can get it back, later," Mom told her softly. "It just stays down in Winnemucca for a while."

"That's your great-grandmother's silver," I said.

"So? It's mine now and I'll pawn it if I like," Mom snapped.

"Stop talking about pawning stuff. We'll get by. I'm taking care of my family," Dad said.

It was definitely time for some real good news around here.

There wasn't any good news at school, either. Killworth taught the two most boring subjects—history and algebra, along with boys' PE—and I was still behind. He was getting deep into World War II, and algebra was getting harder. I was lost and Mom wasn't putting up with bad grades, so I stopped Favi after class one afternoon.

"Can you come over and we'll study history?" I asked.

"I've got a French test tomorrow. Can we do it later?" she said.

"I can't wait. If I don't catch up, Killworth'll have me doing detention, and my mom . . ."

Now Favi isn't known for being a student, but she's smart. She just doesn't let on to most people about her brains. And right then, I'd take any help I could get. "Can you come up tonight?" I asked.

So she walked to our house after dinner. I recalled the times her brother Paco had come over to hang out with Ben when they were in high school and Favi'd tagged along. We always went out by the irrigation ditch to catch bugs or frogs or just to talk. Back then, she had a huge bug collection she kept between paper towels in shoe boxes. Mike and I helped her look for them, but she wouldn't let us kill them. They had to be dead when we found them, which made it harder. Now she sat across from me at the dining room table. "What are you missing?" she asked.

"I got behind about the time he started World War Two."

"So what are your questions?"

"Don't know, I haven't done the reading," I said.

"Well, you won't pass if you don't read."

I knew that. She didn't have to tell me. "There's other stuff I'm doing."

"Well, you aren't boarding with Mike anymore. You might try reading."

"I'm good," I said. I looked out the window.

"Mike says you aren't the same as last year. I told him to let you get used to—everything. But, Cam, he's dying without you to skateboard with. You should get your grades up, just for him."

"I'm doing it, aren't I?" Now I looked at her. I tried to stare her down, but I never could win that game with Favi, so I asked her, "And how's Paco, anyway?" Paco joined up the same time as Ben, but he didn't go to Iraq that first year. "I heard his unit is on its way to relieve some troops in Afghanistan."

"He's okay. He just called last night. They leave next week."

"Sorry," I said. I opened the history book and pretended to read.

"He'll be okay," Favi said. "He's a sharpshooter. He says he'll get off the first shot."

"Sure," I said. But I knew we were both thinking about Ben.

"So, what's the important stuff in this chapter?" I asked.

Favi flipped through the pages of the book. I concentrated on her hand scanning the pages. It's weird how someone who's so annoying some days, can turn around and be as cool to hang out with as she was. "The Korean Conflict," she said. "Read that. I know that will be on the test."

I tried to read it while she memorized French verb tenses. I tried. But how boring do they have to be, going on about battles that happened fifty years ago and expecting me to recall the names of places in Korea?

"I'm switching to algebra," I said.

"I can't help with you that. I got a C on the last test."

"I'll work it out myself." I opened the book and pushed my chair away from the table. I set my mind to the equations and I was glad when Favi went home. I studied better without thinking about her and Paco and Ben.

I figured I'd ask Darrell about the algebra, but the Internet was down, so the next day after school I rode out to find Darrell at the bull ring. He was sitting in the back of his truck, drinking coffee out of a thermos. Steam rose from the plastic cup and a few snowflakes were settling on the brim of his hat.

"Hey, squirt, how's Ben?" he asked.

"He's looking good," I lied.

"You bringing the snow with you?"

"Naw, I haven't learned that trick yet. But I'm working on it." I grinned. "Can you help me with my algebra?"

Darrell jumped off the truck. "Sure. But you help me with this bull first. You can handle the gate."

Even though it was a Tuesday, when the guys met up to practice, it was just Darrell and John, a bullfighter guy from Imlay, who were there on account of the snow. And the bulls didn't look in the best of spirits. They moved close to each other, heads down, getting ready for the storm. I'd never manned the gate. "Okay," I said. "Pick him out."

Darrell picked the little spotted one and waved his hat, moving him into the chute. I tossed the bull rope across the chute and Darrell fixed it on the steer. He was into some serious practice here, in the snow, with just me and John to work the bulls.

We moved the steer into the chute and Darrell climbed the rails. "Let him loose when I'm ready and watch him when I come off." He dropped onto Spotty and nodded his head.

I swung the gate back. Now, professional rings, they have chutes for the left-handed bulls and different chutes for the right-handed ones. Bulls have a favorite direction they turn out of the chute. You can load 'em according to their habit, the gate swings open in the right direction, and that way nobody gets squashed in the process. But the Salt Lick chute was right-handed and Spotty, that day, favored left. The steer stepped back toward the rails and then he and Darrell turned out almost on top of me, forcing me to take a couple of hops up the fence. Spotty made a jump himself and then he bucked hard. Darrell was solid on his back. It was a good ride, and it only ended when Darrell kicked his leg across the steer's back and let himself drop off. He hit the ground on both feet and then Spotty turned square at him, head down. Oh man, that was my signal. I jumped into the ring, ran along Spotty's side, and threw my hat at his rump. He spun around for me, but I was already on the run. Darrell, too. We vaulted up the rails and landed safe on the other side of the fence. John, the bullfighter, was still working the steer. He jumped in front of Spotty for fun, I'm guessing. "Hang your hat on his horn!" Darrell yelled.

John stretched out to toss his hat like a ring on a merry-go-round, and just as he did it, Spotty caught him with a horn and pulled straight up his leg. The loud *zip* noise told me there was damage. John jumped away, leaving his hat to get stomped. His pants were ripped clean open from his calf to his butt. A big red welt was rising up along his pale leg. Darrell and I busted up laughing.

"So how long was that?" Darrell asked.

"I don't know. Was I the timer, too? I figure it was a good long ride, though."

"The longer the better. I'm riding right through the winter, and when spring comes round, I'm riding Ugly. I can just feel the money in my wallet."

"I bet you'll do it," I said.

"Too bad you're not old enough, squirt. You're a natural, like your brother. If you put yourself to practicing every day, you could try too."

"You're the only one around here stupid enough to do it." And since I'd called him stupid, I followed up by asking a favor. "Can we do my algebra now?"

"Climb in the truck, we'll take a look."

We put Spotty back in his pen, John took off, muttering about the price of jeans, and Darrell and me sat in his truck, out of the wind. I did problems and he chimed in when I missed a sign or factored wrong. The snow began falling hard and the sky turned slate gray, so I took my horse and rode home. Her hooves squeaked on the fresh snow.

I got to the barn and put Pepper in her stall, then started toward the house. I heard Grandpa Roy way before I got to the back door. "You can't sell livestock," he said. "Those cattle are the heart of this ranch."

"No, Dad," my father said, "Land is the heart of the ranch. I'll buy more stock."

I slipped in the back door. They didn't notice me. Grandpa's face was red, and he paced as he talked. "You don't need to do it. The bills can wait. We'll see how the spring calves look." I listened from the hall. As few times as Grandpa Roy got stirred up, I'd learned to stay out of the way.

Dad was heating up himself. "The fall calves were good. We have enough. I'm selling them and paying off this ridiculous motel bill from Washington, DC. It wasn't the Ritz, either, and did you see how much it cost? And come to find out the military would have put us up those first six days." He threw an envelope on the counter in front of Grandpa. "And if we don't pay the credit cards off now, there's the interest—eighteen percent interest. You know we pay as we go. You taught me that. I'm not carrying credit through the spring. I'm selling some of the fall calves, and that's it."

"That's not it. I still own this ranch."

Now that was bad. Grandpa owned the title, but it was our family ranch. We all worked. He was pulling rank on Dad, and I could see it didn't set well. Dad got in the last word. "Paying off the bills is the one thing about this wretched situation that I can do." Then he took his coat and left. Grandpa took his own coat and went out the other door.

"Men," Grandma Jean said from the kitchen. "You'd think they could talk this out instead of yelling. I'll bake a cake. Chocolate. They'll set down at the same table for that." She started laying out flour and eggs and butter like they had power to heal.

"So what bills does Dad have that he's selling the calves?" I asked her.

"It's not so much the one's he's got as the ones he sees coming. He's still paying on the trip back east, and the ranch bills are behind without your mom's paycheck. And who knows what more expense there'll be for Ben later on. He doesn't have any money of his own, you know. He's been sending his extra cash home for the ranch." She wiped her hands on a towel. "It's not right. Parents shouldn't have to choose what to do for an injured child. Ben deserves everything we can do for him."

I must have looked stricken. Grandma Jean cracked an egg and said, "Don't worry, Cam. This ranch takes care of itself. And don't forget the angels." She smiled and whipped the eggs into a froth.

"Too bad angels don't make money," I said.

✤ **CHAPTER** ✤

FOURTEEN

It seemed like I'd done nothing but work—on the ranch or on my lessons—all week. It snowed ten inches and froze solid. Since it was November, there wasn't much chance of it thawing soon. Grandpa and I took a run out to the salt lick to crack the ice on the water troughs and drop loads of hay. The fall calves were dusted with snow, their eyelashes white with the frost. Dad hadn't said anything more about selling them, and Grandpa didn't say either. Grandpa had a soft spot for the little ones we'd doctored and branded with our O'Mara Circle M. So did I. I can't tell you what it's like to hear a cow moo, and then bawl, and yelp, and you turn to see her drop a calf in a willow break. She gets to muttering and licking at it right away, and you feel like an intruder. It's like God himself gave you a peek at how the world should be. That's how I wanted to feel.

But instead, we went back to Palo Alto.

"Why do you have to leave again?" Mike asked over the phone.

"They're making me," I said.

"Can't Ben come here?"

"No," I said. That much I knew. Ben could not come home yet.

"Ask if you can stay. We'll skateboard again. You can use my old one."

"I'll try."

But I had to get past Mom.

"I don't want to go," I said.

"Of course you want to go," Mom corrected me.

"It's creepy down there and boring."

"What's boring about seeing your brother?"

I wasn't telling her. "I'm fine seeing Ben. But it's too cold to swim and there's nothing to do."

Mom sighed. "Okay, take your skateboard. That will entertain you."

All right! My skateboard. "Do you mean that?" I asked.

"Yes, take it. Dad and I will be tied up with the doctors, and it will keep you happy."

Now, I knew Mom was pushing me off, like a phone solicitor, but I'd have my board. And I kind of wanted to see Ben. It worked for me.

I called Mike back. "I have to go," I told him.

"You're never around anymore," he said. "I'm thinking about teaching Favi to skate."

"Right." I laughed. "Like Favi would do that. She'd rather work on that old Volvo of your dad's. Wait till I get my board back. Wait till grades come out. And we'll have plenty of time to board at Thanksgiving, promise."

I rode over with Grandpa Roy. This trip was longer than the last one. There was snow east of Reno, which wasn't bad, but we hit it again crossing Donner Pass. I thought we might sit there all day, waiting for the traffic to move along. Grandpa Roy pumped the windshield with washer fluid to keep it clear, and I watched the snow pile onto the slabs of granite and stunted trees. You can almost touch the quiet when it snows up there. I tried to save it in my mind so I could use it in the city.

It didn't work. As soon as we got down the mountain, the snow switched to rain, which is plenty noisy, and the traffic went nuts. The closer we got to Palo Alto, the more I tightened up. We checked in at the same motel but had two rooms this time. We dumped our stuff and drove to the hospital. Ben was just coming out of his physical therapy session. He looked better, but it was a hard day for his speech. He groped around for words, and he managed, finally, to put them together.

"Hey, bro' . . . look," he said, pointing to his feet.

I eyed his slippers and I thought I saw one move. "Is that—?"

"Yep. A toe move . . . told you." He beamed.

Grandpa took his wheelchair and pushed him toward his room.

"So how long before you can move the rest of it?" I asked.

"Cam, hush," Mom said. "That's good progress, isn't it, Ben?"

"Afraid so. I'm getting better with my hand too. . . . Like Captain Hook," he said to Lali.

Her eyes got round. "He's mean," she said.

"Lollipop, no one could be mean to you," Ben answered. He mussed her hair with his good hand. We got back to his room, and he and I arm wrestled, for real, pressing our elbows on his hospital tray. His movement had come back in his right arm, and he was strong. I didn't have a chance. He pinned me. "I win—still." He grinned.

"I let you," I said, but we both knew I hadn't.

"Hey, remember Matt Burton, my buddy from Georgia?" Ben's words began to come out easier. "They're sending him for an operation. On his face. Next time you see him, he'll look better. Plastic surgeons, they do great stuff."

Mom looked away. I was pretty sure it had to do with Ben's own scars. My throat lumped up. Grandma Jean dealt out a round of poker.

"Let me see those cards," Grandpa Roy said.

"You doubting me?" Grandma asked.

"No, I'm sure of you. Sure you mark those cards. Let's see the corners."

Grandma Jean slapped his hand. "Don't play, then. Lali trusts me." We all busted out laughing. Lali trusts everybody.

Grandma and Grandpa, Lali, and me left the hospital early to let Mom and Dad have time to talk with Ben. Lali fell asleep in the motel room, and I went down to the truck to get my skateboard. "Take the cell phone," Grandpa said. "Don't go far, and call if you need us."

Finally, I was out the door, free, and pumping down the street. The wheels sang in my ears. How long since I'd been loose on my board and with all this concrete? I jumped off the curb. I skated along a main street for a while, but the cars were everywhere, so I turned up a side street. The vibrations from the wheels buzzed up through the board to my feet. A couple of blocks in, I saw two kids on skateboards. One was tall with red hair, and the short one was Asian. I called to them. "Is there a skate park around here?"

"No, we use the parking lot at the mini-mart. They don't care, unless the owner's there."

"So where's that?"

They looked me over. I'm guessing they were trying to figure if I was worth their time. "You any good?" the taller one asked.

"I can ride," I said.

He picked up his board and spun the wheels around. "Where do you live?"

Now this could be tricky. Salt Lick wasn't exactly glamorous. "Nevada," I said.

"Nevaahda?" The way he said it grated on my ears. "What are you doing here?"

"Visiting my brother," I said.

"So where's he live?"

Instead of answering, I started down the street on my board. "Where's that mini-mart?" They got on their boards and swerved around me to lead the way. I followed.

The mini-mart lot was big and almost empty. We drifted around it for a while and then I started doing some tricks. The taller kid stopped to watch. I did a kickflip across the concrete at the front of a parking spot, jumped up on the curb, and cruised to a stop in front of the mini-mart door, right next to the NO BIKES, NO SKATEBOARDS sign.

"So how long are you staying at your brother's house?" he asked.

"Not long, we're leaving tomorrow."

"Well, are you coming back?" he asked. He looked excited, like we could board again.

"Yeah, I'll be back. He's in the VA hospital, getting therapy."

The kid's jaw dropped. "So, what happened to him?"

"An IED hit him in Iraq."

"A what?" the short one asked.

"IED—improvised explosive device. A street bomb."

They both stared at me. "Iraq? No way! How'd he get stuck going over there?"

"It was his orders."

The short kid frowned. "Man, I wouldn't go. You couldn't get me in the army for a million dollars. I might go to Canada."

"They don't make you join the military, stupid," the tall kid said. "Not yet, anyway. This kid's brother had to sign up. That's sick."

I pushed my fingernails into my palms. No one talked like that about Ben. "He's a Marine. He's protecting you."

"Not anymore. He's in the hospital, right?"

"And he got there protecting you."

The tall guy glared at me. "Do you like this war or something?"

"Nobody likes a war, but you can't do anything about it but go fight. So don't you go bad-mouthing what all those guys have done," I snapped.

"What kind of garbage do they teach you in Nevaahda? There's always stuff you can do. How about thinking? Maybe blowing people up doesn't make the world safer. And they'd have a hard time running a war without soldiers, wouldn't they?"

"Lay off of him," the short one said. "His brother's in the hospital."

"You don't know anything about my brother," I said. "Or the others." I thought of Ben pulling Burton out of the house in Baghdad, leaving parts of his buddy's legs behind. "You just don't get it," I said. The metallic taste in the back of my throat told me I was going over the edge. I wondered if it was like the smell Ben said would make you puke. I didn't want to puke. I took off on my board before I punched one of them.

The short kid called after me, "Don't run off. He's right, you know. You can't run a war without soldiers."

I turned around and yelled, "And you wouldn't have a country"—I kicked faster—"or this crummy town without them!" I pushed the board as fast as I could on the flat streets, backtracking to where I'd met the jerks. I wanted to break something, but the only thing I had was my board. Then I saw an orange tree, and the fruit was round and ripe, hanging just over my head. I reached up and grabbed one, then two, and three. I cradled the oranges in my arm until I saw a concrete wall. I smashed those oranges good against the wall. One for the tall kid, one for the short one, and the last one I plastered, hard, for the weaselly scumfaced dirtbag who triggered the bomb that tore up Ben.

FIFTEEN

We visited Ben Sunday morning, and I couldn't get the two skater creeps out of my head. "Can I push you around again?" I asked him.

"Sure," Ben said. We left the rest of the family playing cards in his room. "What's up, bro'?"

"I've got to know. Would you really go back now, if you could?"

"Back to Iraq? Where'd that come from?"

I guessed he'd forgotten our conversation, although he was talking okay today. I hated that. You never knew how he was going to be or what he was going to remember. "Doesn't matter," I said. "But I want you to tell me. Was it worth it?"

Ben turned in his chair and stared at me. "That's a lousy question to ask me. Would I go back? Geez, Cam, don't ask that."

"You would, wouldn't you? You'd go and save guys

like Georgia. You'd do it again, wouldn't you?"

Ben slumped back in the chair. "It stinks. It all really stinks. Yeah, I'd go back. I've got buddies, brothers. They're still there. I'd go. In a minute. But bro', it's crazy over there." He thought for a while. "I remember when I got hit, they were in some buildings we drove by. I can see the street now. We traveled it to get out of town. They were waiting in an empty building. That's where the sound came from. A huge sound. *Boom*." He said it, waving his arm, like an explosion in a cartoon. "It hurt." He pointed to his ears. "Blew me out of the truck, and I landed in the street. I remember that."

I didn't know if I should ask for more. I decided to just listen.

"They hate us, Cam," he said. "We're supposed to be the good guys." His voice trailed off. Finally he said, "That's not all of it. There's Iraqis who come up and thank you. They're scared, and they want us to stay and help. It's confusing. Yeah, get them to put me back the way I was, and I'll go back. I wish the crazy war never started." He leaned his head back, eyes closed, and a line of tears squeezed loose on his cheeks. Mom had warned me he could get emotional from the brain changes. I didn't ask what happened when he landed in the street, although I was dying to know. Instead, I turned the chair and pushed him back to his room.

On the drive home, I read my history book so I didn't have to talk. But instead of answering Killworth's questions about the Korean War, I came up with more of my own. What happened to the guys who fought in Korea? What was it like when their feet froze or they stepped on a mine? Did they share their food with starving people? The words on the page got a life of their own. I pictured mothers peeling bark off trees to feed to their babies, the way cattle do in dead winter. I pictured Lali eating bark. My stomach knotted up, and I decided not to skateboard in Palo Alto anymore.

Monday we had an algebra test. I passed, thanks to Darrell. Then Killworth reviewed our history.

"What were the causes of the Korean War?" he asked.

"The Chinese invaded Korea from the north," Favi said.

"But why?" Killworth asked.

I tuned it out. Killworth didn't have anything worth listening to.

But while I was zoning out, I was remembering all kinds of stuff I'd tried to forget. Like talking to Tom Lehi last year, down at the Grange about his time in World War II. I asked if he liked seeing Italy, and he said there wasn't much to see by the time he got there, so much of it was bombed out. "They called us the 'Can Do' unit. It was a frontline command, first ones in to fight the Nazis." So the natural thing was to ask, wasn't the front line dangerous? Tom said, "There were ten thousand men in my division—the Third Infantry—and by the time the war was over, forty thousand men had been assigned to it. The other thirty thousand, well, they say twenty-five thousand were killed or wounded. Imagine, all of those men."

"What about the other five thousand?"

Tom shook his head. "I don't know, they got reassigned or something. When you're there, you aren't counting."

"So, what about your friends?" I asked.

"There were about ten guys I knew who were there, beginning to end. About ten, that's all I knew of."

That's what Tom Lehi told me when Ben was already gone to Iraq. I didn't tell anyone then. And now I wondered how Ben would answer those same questions.

Grandma Jean was about the only one who I figured would give me a straight answer, so I asked her that night when we were doing the dishes. "What's the sense in people blowing each other up?"

"You mean the war?"

"Yeah, I mean Ben and his buddies. You saw them. They're so messed up. What's the use in that?" I waited for her to think. I knew she wouldn't lie to me.

"They're the lucky ones, you know," she said softly. "They survived, and the doctors know how to keep them alive. In other wars, even in Vietnam, if your brother was hurt like that, he would have died."

"Ben doesn't seem so lucky to me."

She took her hands out of the dishwater and dried them off. She looked at me level, her eyes shiny and dark under the soft wrinkles of her eyelids. "Right or wrong, there's nothing glorious about a war. So many people lose everything—their lives, their loved ones, their arms. It happens the same to people on both sides," she whispered. "The suffering is terrible. Your brother's lucky to be home."

"What if he'd been killed?" I asked.

"He wasn't," she said.

"But he could have been."

"Cam, you have to trust that the Lord doesn't take anyone until He's good and ready, and when the time comes, it comes. There's a reason, especially if it's someone young like Ben. He's got a better plan for him."

"Do you believe that?" I asked.

"I do," she said. "Think of your cousin, Adam, drowned when he was only a child. What reason is there for that? But since he's gone, I feel him near me every day. Ben's got more to do on this earth, and Adam, he was needed in heaven."

I dried the iron skillet and put it in the drawer under the stove. Grandma Jean was like that pan, solid and honest. I just wish I could be as sure as she was.

The phone rang and I picked it up. It was Darrell.

"We got a bull ride going at Elko Saturday," he said. "A couple of us are driving over. You want to come?"

"I can't do that, man," I said.

"What's wrong with a drive to Elko? You got something else going? Or won't your mom let you out of town?"

I looked around the kitchen. Ben was gone, Mike was weird since I'd started bull riding, and Favi just wanted to talk about what was bothering me. My mom had my skateboard in her closet again until my grades came up. Nothing seemed right since Ben got hurt except the rush I got on the back of a bull. The phone line was dead quiet.

"So, you coming?" Darrell asked.

"Yeah, I am. For sure."

✶ CHAPTER ✶

SIXTEEN

Lying to my folks was easier than I'd hoped it would be. I just said I was driving with Darrell to Elko, where he was picking up a motor off a guy he knew. Mom had always liked Darrell, and she even packed us a lunch—roast beef and horseradish sandwiches and a bag of corn chips to hold Grandma Jean's tomatillo salsa. The good thing was, we were fixing to bull ride a hundred miles away from Salt Lick. There was no way anyone would see me there.

It was the kind of day you remember and keep looking back on, wondering if it was as good as you thought or if somehow it was so good it was bad. We started out before sunrise. Darrell turned up the radio full blast. We had a thermos of coffee and the road was clear and dry. The sun rose after we'd turned east from Winnemucca, and the light flashed off the snowy mountains. The air was perfect, clear like glass.

"I brought an extra bull rope for you," Darrell said.

"We're going to get you scored today. It don't do to keep you practicing without knowing what you might be able to do."

"But I just started," I said.

"Yeah, and you're too old to start riding and too young to be as good as you are. You just rode two tough bulls. You're something, Cam, anybody can see that. Time to see what the judges think."

I took a long swig of coffee and smiled.

We got to Elko midmorning and Darrell drove us to his friend's ranch. The pickups and horse trailers were already coming in. I saw some license plates from as far off as Utah and Idaho.

"So is this a big deal?" I asked.

"Just friends getting together before the winter sets in. We do some bull riding, roping, and stuff. Steve's been throwing this for years. I told him you were coming."

"You didn't know that," I said. Darrell grinned and I thought maybe it wasn't just Grandpa and Ben who were stubborn—maybe it was bull riders. Maybe bull riders figured things always turned out the way they wanted.

We parked and headed toward the corral. There was a big bald man there with a clipboard. "Steve, this is my boy, Cam, the one I told you about. You know, he's Ben O'Mara's brother."

Steve reached for my hand and pumped it. "Ben O'Mara's one heck of a bull rider. I can't wait to see you in action. How's Ben doing, anyway?"

"As well as you'd think," I said. Did everyone know Ben?

"Well, you give him my regards, okay? That was a tough turn he took. Tell him we're thinking of him. I've got you up fifth." He looked me over. "You're old enough, right?"

I was about to ask, old enough for what? when Darrell said, "'Course he's old enough. I wouldn't bring any kids out here. He graduates this year, right? If they let him." Darrell grinned.

Steve eyed me. "Well, you're sure tall enough to fill the bill. Got some shoulders on you too." He looked me over like he was summing up a steer at auction. "This ain't school, so we don't care." He elbowed me and winked. "Just as long as you're eighteen and old enough to take your own chances. I don't need anybody's parents suing me."

"Mine won't," I said. Mom would kill me first.

The Elko bull ring had a left- and a right-handed chute. There were some folks there selling Indian tacos out of the back of a trailer and some others who'd brought sleazy T-shirts to sell that said "Bull Buster" and "Eight Seconds of Heaven." There was a barrel in the ring for the bullfighters to dodge behind if they got in a tight spot, and some makeshift bleachers along the side. Two old guys sat at a table midway round the ring. I figured them to be the judges. The timer had an air horn to call the eight seconds. The cowboys were lining up with their gear. Steve might have believed Darrell—that I was old enough to do this—but I felt young. Real young. It didn't matter that I was the only guy in my class who actually had to shave every week. And I could skip that too, except for the black whiskers I got from the Carl side of the family. No, all these guys looked confident and cool. Could they see how nervous I was? Darrell handed me his second bull rope. I had that feeling again—that sane men would leave.

I looked over the stock jammed into the holding corral. It seemed like they'd picked them for their size. I turned to Darrell. "They're pretty big."

"Nothing bigger than Quicksand."

"Yeah, right. Nothing bigger than that monster," I said. "Do you think I can score?"

"Shut up," he said. "It's bad luck to talk about it."

"Don't worry, kid," a graying cowboy said to me. "Ain't nothing a bull can do to you that a two-ton truck can't." He laughed.

I didn't feel any better. I pushed my hands into my jacket pocket and felt something smooth and small. I pulled out Grandma Jean's little packet of good-luck stuff. I reached inside and felt the baggie of Salt Lick salt. I put the whole packet into my jeans and hoped Grandpa was right—that the salt worked magic with bulls.

The stands held a handful of folks from the cowboys' families. Steve turned on a microphone; a sturdy woman raised the American flag while we held our hats over our hearts. Then Steve announced, "Our first rider today is all the way from Nampa, Idaho. Let's hear it for Jesse Spellman on Snowball."

A big albino bull came out of the chute, but he was running instead of bucking. Then he kicked a couple of times and finally started to buck. Jesse was spurring him, but the bull was lazy. Jesse got a reride. See, the scoring goes fifty points for how bad the bull is to ride and fifty more for how good the cowboy rides him. You have to stay eight seconds to score at all. In this ride, Snowball didn't do his part.

Next was a big, sunburned cowboy on a black-and-white bull. The bull was heavier than most, but you could still see his muscles move. I was standing by the fence, as I'd be fixing my bull rope soon—close enough to see the cowboy fall and hear his bone snap when he hit the ground. The bullfighters jumped in to distract the bull, and a couple of guys pulled the rider out of the ring, raising a dust cloud behind him. They set him down next to me, and someone poked around at his collarbone. He reached up to his shoulder and rocked, just a little, back and forth. His moans mixed in with the cattle's mooing. It hit me, what if I broke something? What would I say to Mom and Dad then?

"That's a tough break for a tough cowboy," the announcer said. "We'll let you know when we have word what's happening. Meantime, there's another bull coming down the chute, and this one belongs to Seth Yoman."

I watched them unbutton the downed cowboy's shirt, and before they finished taping his shoulder, a woman came running over.

"You all right?" she called. "Don't tell me you broke something again."

He muttered, "I'm good," and stood up, although the color drained from his face.

"Well, after you wrecked your back last time, I was afraid . . ." The woman's voice tapered off to a whisper.

"It's just a bull," he said. "Nothing's gonna happen." But I could tell from her face, she didn't believe him.

"You're next," someone said to me. I hadn't watched Yoman. I didn't even know if he scored, but it was my turn to ride. I drew a red bull with a white face and thick horns.

He was stocky and his hair swirled in stiff cowlicks on his back. He bawled when they moved him into the chute. I climbed up to the platform, tossed Darrell's bull rope under him, and cinched it tight. Then I waited. As the seconds passed, I kept hearing the snap of the guy's shoulder bone.

"Next we have a young cowboy come up from Salt Lick. He's from a bull-riding family—you might know his grandpa Roy, or big brother, Ben. And now he's out to put his own name in the record books. Let's give a big hand to Cam O'Mara on Rosy." I barely heard the applause. "Cam O'Mara" was what I heard. What a rush to hear my name over the mike—even if it was in the same sentence with Ben's.

"Time to ride," a cowboy said to me. "Make your brother proud."

I shook my head fast side to side to shake out his words like a curse. Geez, did they always have to put me up against Ben? I lowered myself onto Rosy and tried to put the *crack* of the big cowboy's bone out of my mind. I drew in Rosy's smell, roughed my rope, and felt him rock under me. "Let 'im go," I said, and we took off.

You can think before you get on a bull, and you can think after you fall off, but when you are on, you just ride. I rode till I heard an air horn, then I ripped my rope and fell to the ground. I spit dust and crawled up to my feet. Rosy trotted around to the other end of the ring, so I walked to the fence.

"O'Mara gets the first score. Seventy with Rosy."

"All right, Cam!" Darrell whooped. I saw him in the back, waiting for his ride. Seventy wasn't exactly a high score. The bull was easy. But it was my first score, and it felt great. Darrell rode and got an eighty-two. Andrew Echevarria showed up and didn't score on his first round. Then I rode the albino, Snowball, and didn't score either. Darrell's second score was eighty, and Andrew got eighty-eight. Then it was done. They started the calf roping, and we bought chewy Indian tacos from a kid in the trailer and watched the action in the arena. The whole day just flew by. Then the stock was ready to load into the cattle trucks, and the cowboys were breaking out the beer.

"To one crazy sweet day," Darrell said.

I had to agree.

SEVENTEEN

I sat with Mike on the bus after school on Monday. "Report cards are coming out," Mike said. "Do you think you'll get your skateboard back?"

"Yeah. I'm getting A's and B's now. That should be enough to cut it loose from Mom."

"Come over when you get it. We can practice some new tricks. I found these cool skate videos online."

"I'll have to do my homework first."

"Man, it's always something with you," Mike said. "Get your mom to let you out. If your grades are as good as you say, you've earned it. Come on, you're the only one around that's fun to board with. I've waited a long time."

"Me too," I said.

I raced home from the bus. I skipped up the porch steps, swung through the door, and asked, "Are report cards here?"

Mom looked up from her accounting and quietly

pointed to the envelope. There they were, my A's and B's. My afternoons studying with Favi and my tutoring with Darrell. My pass to skateboarding. To Mike's house. To my regular life.

"Congratulations," Mom said.

"Do I get my board back now?"

Mom took off her reading glasses and set them on her papers. "We need to talk."

"About what? I brought my grades up."

"About bull riding. Oscar says you've been bull riding."

"How would he know?" I asked.

She raised her eyebrows. "Are you saying he's lying? Is it a different Cam O'Mara he's talking about?"

Favi must have said something to her father. Or maybe her uncle told him or one of the guys from Elko. I forgot to breathe.

Mom went on. "I know you've been bull riding and so you aren't getting your skateboard. And you aren't off restriction. And since we can't trust you on weekends around here, your dad and I have decided you'll come with us to Palo Alto."

"This weekend?" I asked.

"Every weekend until we think different."

"You can't do that! I brought my grades up, you owe me my board."

"Cam, when you act like this, I don't think we owe you anything."

I grabbed my report card, tore it up, and tossed it in the wastebasket. It was too good for them. I went out to the barn to blow off some steam. I put a halter on one of the yearlings and ran him around the corral until I broke a sweat, and then I kept running.

Neil Jones pulled up in his truck. "Where's your dad, Cam?"

"Haven't seen him."

"Well, when you do, tell him I came by to look at that stock he's selling. He said they're the ones in the back corral, right?"

"I don't know," I said. It surprised me that Dad was going ahead selling the stock. If Grandpa Roy found out about it, he would chase Mr. Jones right off the ranch. Those calves were O'Mara calves, with our brand. And I wasn't feeling much like helping Dad sell them. I believed what Grandpa said about selling stock cutting at the heart of the ranch— being the beginning of the end. The way things happened lately, losing the ranch wouldn't take long from start to finish. "I don't think they're for sale," I said.

"Really? But your dad called."

"You better talk to my grandpa," I said. "Ask him. He'll know."

Now, I knew right then that I'd messed with a big sale and the money for our bills. Money Mom and Dad might need for Ben. I knew Grandpa wouldn't sell the calves. And right then, I didn't care.

"I saw his truck. Is he in the house?" Mr. Jones asked.

"Yeah," I said. And then I couldn't take it back.

So there wasn't any reason for me to spend the weekend before Thanksgiving in Salt Lick, even if Mom would have let me. I couldn't skateboard, and Mike was steamed.

Grandpa and Dad were hardly talking after the calf deal fell through. Mom was crazy as a dog on a scent about me and the bull riding. So it felt right, like the punishment fit me, to pack my duffel bag and sit silent in the backseat of the truck while we crossed the mountains and went back to California. Okay, so Ben was messed up, but at least he'd probably talk to me.

The motel was the same. Mom and Dad were the same. The crowds were the same. But Ben seemed different. He was talking better, and they'd fitted him for another temporary arm and were fixing on getting his skull put back together with an operation right after Christmas. You'd think that would cheer him up, but he was majorly down. I didn't feel much like cheering anybody up, but I gave it a try.

"So where's Burton?" I asked.

"Burton? They sent him back east for that surgery and then he's going home."

"Oh," I said. "That's good, right? He gets to go home?"

"Yeah." Ben stared at the wall. I searched around for something to talk about.

"Is there anyone else from your unit here? Anybody you know from over there?"

Ben took his time answering. "Yeah, one guy came in last week. . . . Two more of 'em didn't make it this far."

"What do you mean?" I asked.

"They ambushed my unit again. It was a couple of grenades that took 'em out." He looked away. "It can tear a person up when one of those goes off at close range. I should have been there."

"So, are your friends dead?"

"One wounded. Two dead. Like before." Ben's face was taut. "I should have been there," he repeated softly. "I could have done something for them."

"Ben, you said there wasn't much left. . . . You'd be dead too. You can't save everybody."

"No, but I'm supposed to be there, not in this hospital. What good is that?"

"It'll be real good when you get your new skull and come home. You'll see. Things'll be good again."

"You think so?" He looked expectant, waiting for my answer, like a little kid.

"Sure," I said, and I put my hand on his. "Mom says the doctors want you to remember stuff. You want to talk about the dumb stuff we did when we were kids?"

"Like when you, me, and Grandma Jean TP'ed Pastor Fellows's house?" he asked.

"Yeah, or when Grandpa Roy got mad at us for running the cows around the salt lick because I wanted to see how fast they could go."

"I don't remember that," Ben said.

"Sure you remember. Grandpa was so mad I though his face would burst."

"You gotta think of the cattle first," Ben said. He could still quote Grandpa Roy.

"So, what *do* you remember?" I asked.

He thought. Finally, he said, "I remember when Adam Carl drowned."

"You do? I don't remember that."

"You were too young. But I was there. It was Adam's birthday, and he and I were in a rowboat on Walker Lake.

Some bees came around, and he took off his life vest and dove in to get away from them. He splashed me, and we were laughing. Grandma Jean yelled at us to come in. But I jumped in the lake too. That's when Adam slipped under the water. I thought he was playing."

"So, what did you do?"

"Nothing," he said. "Same as now. Only back then, I thought he was playing."

Nobody'd ever told me that Ben had been there. "You didn't know," I said. Ben was crying. I handed him a tissue. "Grandma Jean says the Lord doesn't take kids unless there's a good reason."

"Right," Ben said.

"There had to be a reason," I said.

"Right."

EIGHTEEN

Thanksgiving came around, but I wasn't feeling too thankful. It was harder having Ben in the hospital than it was the year before when he was gone in Iraq. Mom wanted the holiday at home, "like normal," and we were all hauling ourselves back to Palo Alto on Friday to visit Ben. Dad carved the turkey, and Mom served up the potatoes and stuffing.

"I wish Jones had bought those fall calves," Dad said.

I smoothed the wrinkles out of the fancy cloth napkin in my lap.

"He knows he ain't doing you no favors taking your stock," Grandpa Roy said. "That's your future income. Sell them when they're fat, and we'll have more money."

Dad scowled. "He wanted the calves. And no one else has been round to look at them. I'll have to take them down to auction."

I twisted the corner of the napkin tight around my finger.

Grandpa grunted. "They aren't bidding up at auction this winter. Take them in spring."

"I'll get my job back," Mom said quietly.

Dad turned pale. "Don't do that, Sherry. You don't know when Ben will need you. We'll work something out."

Now Grandma Jean chimed in. "Honey, you have plenty to do with the ranch and the children and your bookkeeping. You'll put yourself in an early grave if you start back to work, too. And I have to get back home to Hawthorne one of these days. I won't be here to help you."

Of all of it, that was the worst. "You don't have to go back, do you?" I asked her.

"Pretty soon, Cam. Your Aunt Shawna's been stopping by my house, but I should look after my own place. And I'll be wanting to come back when Ben gets home for good. That's when you'll need more help."

"But you live *here* now," Lali said. "We have more books to read."

"You're getting to be a good reader yourself, and I'll write you letters and you can write back."

Lali stuck out her lip. "Will they come to the mailbox? Can I open them myself?"

"Yes, they will." Grandma Jean smiled.

"All right," Lali said. "Pass the Jell-O salad, please."

After dinner, we went to the Baptist hall for the annual dessert and prayer meeting. Pastor Fellows started it when I was little so some of the old-timers could share a Thanksgiving meal without feeling like they were taking a handout from their neighbors. Mike's dad drove their Suburban around to the old folks' places, put a step stool on the ground, and collected them up. All of Salt Lick came, didn't matter if they were Baptist or not, 'cause this was the closest we got to a town party all year.

The desserts were always great—German chocolate cake, Basque flan, and all kinds of cookies. Grandma Jean and Lali had baked three kinds of pies themselves, and Grandpa Roy bought ten gallons of vanilla ice cream last time he was in Winnemucca at the Savers Club.

"You can bring that pie straight into the kitchen, and we'll get it served up," Grandma Jean said to me.

I felt the heat from all the people in the hall as we passed through. There were only a few women in the kitchen, and Grandma Jean offered for me to scoop out the ice cream. I rolled up my sleeves and dug in, happy for something to do. When I had about three dozen scoops, we loaded some trays and started carrying them out to the tables.

Darrell waved me over. "How's Ben?"

"Okay, I guess. We saw him last week. He can move his toes, and now they say he can wiggle his foot."

Darrell looked away. "His foot, huh? Is that all he can do?"

I felt the need to explain. "No, that's really good. It means he might walk. That's what they say. It's all good. You should go see him in Palo Alto."

"I'm not much for cities. And Ben don't want me to see him laid up and sittin' around in his pajamas."

"He doesn't wear pajamas all day."

"Well, I'll come by when he's home in Salt Lick." Darrell

brightened up. "So when are you coming back to the bull ring?"

"Shhh." I shook my head. "I can't. My folks are watching me all the time. It's making me nuts."

I took some ice cream over to Mike and Favi and sat down with them.

"What's up?" Mike asked.

"Nothing," I said.

"I'm taking my driver's test Monday. Then I can drive you *unlicensed* teens around." He grinned.

"No, you can't," I said. "You can just drive your mom around."

"What *is* up with you?" Mike asked.

"Something's up," Favi said. "Why is your father trying to sell off calves early?"

Why did Favi always have to know everything? I rested my head in my hands. "We could use the money," I said.

"I've got an idea," Favi said. "You could go into AI breeding like Amy Jones. You can store up the AI straws from each bull in the freezer and then if a bull wins a big prize and goes out of service, you can sell his straws for ten or twelve thousand dollars *apiece*. That's good money." Then she thought a moment. "But you have to have money to buy your straws in the first place."

"I said we were short on money, not that Dad was looking to spend more." But Favi was right about Jones making big money. Amy shipped those little AI straws around the world. Honest. The folks who bought them used them to sire calves, and they didn't have to truck the bull in from Montana or Texas or wherever to have his day with the cows. But like Favi said, getting started with the equipment and all is expensive.

"I know," Mike said. "You could ride that bull, Ugly, that Darrell keeps talking about. That'd win you some money." He made his fingers like horns.

Favi laughed. "Yeah, if you can ride him and you don't break your neck."

I shook my head. "You guys are crazy. I'm not doing that."

About then, Pastor Fellows stood up to start the prayers. He prayed for the old and infirm—that included Ben. He prayed for sinners. After messing up the calf sale, I figured that was me. He prayed for the folks who ran everything from the town recycling to the whole United States. Then we started the thanksgivings—everyone said something out loud. Lali said thanks for her goat, Pretty, and for the letters she was going to get right in our mailbox. Grandma Jean blessed our family, and Mom said she was thankful that Ben was getting better. I didn't hear Grandpa Roy or Dad because I was too busy thinking up my own speech. Was I thankful that Ben was alive—and messed up? That I'd ridden some bulls—and couldn't tell anybody? That Grandma Jean made me laugh—and now she was going away? When my turn came around, I passed.

Mike and I didn't skateboard over Thanksgiving like I'd promised him. The next day, our whole family left for California at three in the morning. Grandma Jean came with us in her Bronco. She was packed to go straight on back to Hawthorne from there. We got to the hospital in early afternoon. The nurses' station was decorated with turkeys and big cut-out leaves. Lali gave them a picture of a turkey she'd drawn on the trip across the mountains, and they hung it up like a Picasso painting. Then we all went in to see Ben. It was like I'd never left.

"Hi." He smiled at Mom. He showed Lali his new arm and she rubbed on it.

"It's smooth," she said. "And hard. I thought they'd make you a real arm."

"My real one's gone," Ben said.

Grandpa tried to talk to him about the cows and bulls, but Ben wasn't having much of it. He kept dropping off to sleep. The rest of the family all decided to go to the canteen for some food, but I said I'd stay with Ben. I could use some time without everybody else.

"You still here?" he asked when he woke up.

"Yeah, you're stuck with me."

"I'm not much company," he said, rolling away from me.

"So, how you feeling?"

"Fine."

"Did they give you turkey yesterday?"

"I don't remember," he mumbled. I'm guessing he did remember and he didn't want to talk, although I suppose he could've forgotten, too. I wished Grandpa Roy had stayed behind. He'd have got him talking. Or Grandma Jean, she'd do something to make him laugh. I looked around the hospital room. It's not your funniest place. There were water cups and paper towels, a spit tray, and some glass doohickeys. Then I spotted the rubber gloves. I pulled one out of the box and blew it up. The fingers fanned out like a chicken balloon. I tied off the bottom.

"What are you doing?" Ben asked.

"Making you a turkey. Seems like you need a turkey."

"It needs eyes," Ben said. "There's a marker in that drawer."

I drew eyes on the turkey and made another one and another one. I piled them up in Ben's lap. "I'm making you a whole flock of turkeys," I said. I found some adhesive tape and started taping them to the walls.

"That's a lot of turkeys," Ben said.

"There's a lot of turkeys in the world," I answered. "Here." I took the marker and wrote names on them. "This one's Mr. Killworth. And this one's for the credit-card company that's bugging Dad. What about you, Ben? What name do you want on a turkey?"

"I don't know."

"Sure you do," I pushed him.

"Nobody. Everybody's great."

"You don't act like everybody's great."

And right then he let out with a line of insults and vinegar that I couldn't write down on the stupid glove turkeys if I tried. He covered everybody from Hitler to Saddam Hussein, from the therapist who stretched on his legs till they hurt to a nurse who wouldn't give him chocolates. He went nuts with the turkey list. Finally he said, "And the rat-faced piece of scum who shot me." Exactly how do you get that on a glove?

"Wow," I said.

"I'm sorry," he whispered.

By the time they came back, Ben was asleep again and I handed the turkeys to Lali. She drew feathers over the names.

That night in the motel, Grandma Jean woke me up. "You need some fun," she said. "Come on." We snuck outside and she pointed to a big blue spruce in the circle in front of the motel. It was the only living thing in a swath of concrete. "They need some holiday spirit and so do you," she said. And, as if by magic, she pulled Christmas lights and candy canes out of her big rose-covered bag. She opened the back of the Bronco and pulled out some garish red Christmas balls.

"You planned all this, Grandma," I said.

"We had to do something fun before I left," she whispered. "Now, see how far you can get up that tree."

The motel people were asleep and no one driving by seemed to notice an old lady and a kid in his pajamas climbing around in the motel tree with Christmas decorations. The branches were prickly, but I didn't mind. Once again, Grandma Jean came through. With her around, I didn't need angels.

NINETEEN

G randma Jean went home, and about ten days later we made one more trip to Palo Alto before Christmas. This time Mom and Dad stayed home with Lali and I drove over with Grandpa Roy.

"Are we staying in the same place?" I asked. Maybe they had seen me and Grandma Jean.

"Why do you ask?" Grandpa Roy looked over at me.

"No reason," I said. I fussed with the zipper on my jacket.

"It wouldn't have anything to do with a Christmas tree in the parking lot, would it? Darnedest thing—they decorated that motel in the middle of the night," he said.

"Yep," I answered.

"Must be a city thing," he said.

"Yep." I smiled and looked at him. He was grinning.

"You know, that happened once out at the salt lick. Right about Christmastime. We were pretty sure the cows didn't do it. But your Grandma Jean was in town."

"Really," I said, still smiling. "I wish she hadn't left."

"Life goes on," he said.

"So, what other stuff happened at the salt lick?" I asked. "Tell me one of the stories." Grandpa Roy always had a salt lick story. Of all the old guys who told 'em, Grandpa's were the craziest, 'cause it was his salt, I'm guessing.

Grandpa turned down the radio and settled back. We were driving by the Humboldt Sink, east of Reno, and this early in the morning, we were the only car on the road. "Did I ever tell you about that baby who started talking after his mother put salt from the lick on his crackers?"

"No, I'd remember that one."

"Well, there was this new gal in town, she was wife to a teacher—they didn't last too long, but she had this kind of sickly little baby that she carried around. And in all his life, he never made a sound. She'd had him up to the doctor to see if he was deaf and should go for speech therapy and whatnot. Well, the word was no, he was too young to be talking—about ten months—but he bore watching. That's what they said.

"I saw that baby a couple of times and it was unnatural the way he didn't make a noise at all—not even if he fell over, or if a dog come up and licked him. Well, one day we had a barbecue out at the salt lick, way we did for Ben, you know, and she brought the baby. Somebody gave her some crackers for the baby, but he wouldn't eat them, and sickly as he was, all the women started fussing, trying to get him to eat. Then Neil Jones walks by and says, "Try some salt from the lick. The cows love it." Everybody laughed, but darned if she didn't walk out to the salt lick and break off a hunk of the salt. She crumbled it up over the crackers and the baby sat up and ate 'em all."

"How many did he eat?" I asked.

"Who knows? A lot. It's not pertinent to the story. But what is, is that very day they say the baby started talking. He said, 'Mama' and 'Dada,' and then he started in sentences, and before nightfall they couldn't shut him up. The doctors said he was a child prodigy or some nonsense, and his folks took him off to Reno and San Francisco for tests. But they never found nothing special about him. And we know why. It was the salt they needed to be testing, not the kid." Grandpa slapped the steering wheel and laughed.

"That all true?" I asked.

"'Course it's true." His blue eyes twinkled.

"Yeah, they're always true," I said.

"Darn right."

Our Christmas tree was still up at the motel, and Grandpa remarked on what fine decorations it had when we checked in. The clerk just looked uncomfortable and gave us the key to our usual room. I would have been just fine hanging out there and watching cable TV. But Grandpa was ready to see Ben.

I have to admit, I was kind of afraid to see him. I never knew what he was going to do, and I would've been just as happy letting him do it alone and getting him back when he was more like the Ben I knew. No such luck. We put down our bags and went straight over to the hospital.

Ben was doing water therapy, and we waited for him to finish. Then we took him for a ride around the hallway. Somebody had wrapped boxes and hung them on the walls like Christmas packages.

"Anything happen lately?" I asked.

"No."

"How's the therapy?" Grandpa asked.

"Okay."

"Did you hear from Burton?" I asked.

"No, he's gone home."

The wheels of his chair hummed against the floor. A guy went by with a walker and the *galump* sound of his contraption followed him. A kid walked by.

"Stop," Ben said. "Did you see that kid?"

"Not really," Grandpa said.

"He looks familiar," Ben said. "I don't know why."

"You've probably seen him around with his family," Grandpa said.

"He looks like a kid I saw selling Indian tacos last month in Elko," I said.

"I wish I could remember." Ben looked worried. "I wish I could remember stuff like that."

We turned into his room. "They're working on my memory, and some things are coming back. I remember more about when I got hit."

Grandpa cocked his head. "And?"

"After I got blown out of the truck, I was bleeding. The pain in my arm took over. It's the worst—the pain just hammered me. I could see my bones sticking through my skin. I started yelling, but nobody was coming for me, and they were still shooting. I thought someone might finish me off. I needed to play dead. I wanted to scream from the pain, but I just put my head down, bit my lip, and lay there."

"Then what happened?" I asked.

"I don't know," he said. "I got out of there somehow, but nobody knows how."

"Somebody knows," Grandpa said. "You'll remember."

"Sure," Ben said. And just like that, he asked us to get him over to his bed. He was getting pretty good with the arm he had left. He grabbed the bed rail and dragged himself toward the bed. Grandpa moved fast and pushed on his hip the way he did at home. Ben slid into the bed, turned away from us, and said, "I'm tired now."

"Anything we can get you?" Grandpa asked.

"Bring me two legs that work, okay? And an arm—like the last one." He didn't sound like he was joking.

I messed around with his pillows and filled his water glass. I put some magazines on the bedstand.

"We'll come back later," Grandpa Roy said.

"Later," Ben answered, and waved us out of his room.

I wanted to run down the hall, but I matched Grandpa Roy's gait. We were almost to the door when one of the nurses caught up to us. "Are you visiting Ben O'Mara?"

"Yes, ma'am," Grandpa said.

"Listen, you are family, right? You should know that he's getting depressed. We're trying to work with him, but the therapy is slow. And it's tiring. They can go out into the community here, and they're still looking for snipers on overpasses, or they won't walk past a certain kind of doorway. I don't suppose he talks about it. These guys can keep a stiff upper lip for so long and then it gets to them, if you know what I mean?"

Grandpa Roy nodded.

"He could use whatever you can do to cheer him up. We're doing our best here. They are wounded warriors and they're proud of what they've done. They're so proud. Ben had such high hopes because of the foot movement. But he's impatient. It goes with the TBI. He has to keep working until he gets to a breakthrough. Sometimes the guys run out of hope before that happens and then it's so hard to continue. And it's the holidays, too. Just ask your family to do whatever they can to support him now, okay?"

Grandpa looked straight at her and said, "He's a bull rider, you know. He's not scared of sixteen hundred pounds of animal. I'm thinking he'll make it through this."

TWENTY

What that nurse said was the first thing on my mind when we got home. "Ben's really down. He was in a nasty mood," I said.

"He's not himself," Mom said.

"The nurse said we need to keep him going till he gets a breakthrough. Mom, he feels real bad."

"Oh," her face fell. "I'm so sorry."

"I was thinking, instead of going over there for Christmas, can we bring him here?"

"He's not finished at the VA yet," Dad said.

"But he *could* come home, just for a while."

"The boy's right," Grandpa Roy said. "Ben's in some trouble over there."

Mom said, "Oh, Jim, we could have Christmas the way we always do. I'd love to have him here."

Dad put his arm around her. "Call and ask, then. It won't hurt to ask."

— ✷ —

So we didn't have Christmas in a motel room or the Fisher House, where some families of the wounded can stay for free. We didn't drive to Palo Alto with a wreath and little pumpkin pies baked in muffin tins, like Mom had planned. No, instead, Dad and Lali cut a tree up Sugar Canyon. Mom strung popcorn and cranberries for it like when we were kids, and Lali drew a bunch of ornaments on cardboard that looked like stars and goats and cows. I threw the tinsel on. Of course, there were lights and glass Christmas balls too, and candy canes and ribbon bows and pine cones covered with glitter that we'd made in Sunday school ages ago.

Three days before Christmas, Mom and Dad flew to California and brought Ben back to Reno on the plane, then drove to the ranch. It was your regular Christmas get-together, unless you counted the hospital bed in our living room next to the tree. By now Dad and Grandpa Roy had built a ramp for Ben's wheelchair, and Grandma Jean sent a box of sweatpants she'd sewn up with handles on the right side so Ben could pull 'em up easier one-handed.

This time, when Ben came home, I wasn't scared of how his body'd be. I knew about that. It was his mind that worried me. Turned out, all the surprises weren't wrapped up. TBI doesn't act the way you think. After just three weeks without seeing him, when Ben opened his mouth to talk, it was like he was almost back where he ought to be. "Hey, bro'," he said. "Merry Christmas. I would have brought you a present but they were all out of Barbie dolls."

"I want a Barbie," Lali said.

"I bet you do, Lollipop, and Santa's bringing some special stuff, just for you."

Wow, Ben hadn't said that much all in one breath and that easily since he was hit. How you figure it, I don't know, but I was thankful for the miracle. We all were and everybody talked to him all at the same time.

Ben still couldn't walk. "I'm working on it," he said. "They've got a machine I pump on every day. It's not half as fun as riding a bull, though." Grandpa rolled Ben's wheelchair up next to the Christmas tree. "I've got something to show you," Ben said. He pulled his jacket sleeve back, and there, bright as day, was a new left arm. This one had a hand like a mannequin's instead of a hook. He made the thumb and finger move back and forth. It didn't look half bad.

"Pretty cool, huh? This is my permanent one. I've got another new one with a hook, too. I can do more with that one."

"Can I touch it?" Lali asked.

"Sure, Lollipop, touch it," he said.

She rubbed the back of Ben's new hand. "It's softer than the last one. This one's better." She kissed him on the cheek.

Nothing had felt as good in a long, long time as the messing around we did that afternoon. The sun set early, and we fed the animals in the dark. When I came in, Ben was watching TV. "So, Ben, what do you want for Christmas?" I asked. "Don't matter, anyhow. I already got your present."

"I don't think you can get me what I want."

"Try me," I said.

He spoke softly. "I want to get back to my unit. I want my

legs to work. They say my brain might still do it."

"If anybody's brain can do it, it's yours."

"I just can't focus. And I'm no good to do anything around here." He changed the channel. "Okay, I just have to try harder." His glared at the TV like he was getting mad. I'd seen his mood swings in the hospital, and I needed to do something.

"Look at that," I said. "*Miracle on Thirty-Fourth Street.* Remember that movie? They hauled in all those bags of mail for Santa Claus and poured 'em right on the judge's desk. Cool, right?"

"Yeah, cool," Ben said. "Remember when you wrote to Santa for a puppy?"

"Sure, and he brought me my dog, Red, just like I asked."

"Good ol' Santa," he said. "You thought he'd forgotten till Mom told you she'd heard reindeer walking around the barn."

"That's where my puppy was hiding," I said. Then I stopped. "You *remember*?" I asked.

Slowly, Ben's face lit up. "Yeah, I suppose I do."

Christmas was great. It snowed overnight and Lali about busted a gut over her new bike. We gave Grandpa Roy a fancy bridle, the kind for parades and whatnot. Grandma Jean carried that yarn around in her big bag for a reason. All the while she'd been staying with us, she'd knitted up a pile of sweaters, and now she sent one for everybody. Mine didn't even have reindeer or snowflakes on it. It was a plain deep green. You'd actually want to wear it.

I gave Ben a phone card and some CDs. There's not much you can really use in the hospital. He gave me a lead rope he'd braided in his occupational therapy class.

"How'd you make that?" I asked.

"Slowly," he laughed. "The therapist helped."

"Thanks, man."

"No worries, bro'."

Ben saved his present for Mom for the last. It was a little box wrapped in shiny green paper. She unwrapped it, lifted the lid, and ran her finger across whatever was inside. She brushed a tear off her cheek.

"Don't cry, Mom," he said. "I really want you to have it."

Mom wiped her eyes and handed the box to Dad. He turned it face out so we could see. Right there, sitting on a square of velvet, was Ben's Purple Heart—the medal the government gives guys who get wounded in wars. "I wouldn't be here . . . I needed you there, Mom . . . all that time," Ben said to her. "I don't remember much." He grinned. "But I want you to know . . ."

Mom clutched the tiny medal to her heart. Then she kissed Ben on his helmet.

Ben stayed with us for two more days and then his leave was over, and Mom and Dad flew him back. Talking to him, joking with him over Christmas, it was like waking up from a really, really bad dream.

The holiday season seemed to soften Mom up, and she gave me back my skateboard and took me off restriction. Favi was in Mexico with her family, and Mike's family took a vacation in Hawaii, so I spent my freedom hanging out with Lali. We piled dirt and gravel into a low ring, like a dam, behind the barn. I hooked up the hose and filled it with water.

"It's almost done, Cammy." Lali clapped her hands.

"Not yet. It'll be ready tomorrow."

It froze overnight, and the next day, we had a sheet of ice to slide around on.

And since Mom had to drop some bookkeeping jobs on account of the extra time she'd spent with Ben in Palo Alto, Dad cut back on more expenses. He sold some old equipment but he didn't sell any stock. He probably didn't fancy going up against Grandpa Roy again.

Grandpa Roy had let me drive the pickup and the ATVs and tractors around the ranch since I was about ten, so now I asked my folks if I couldn't drive into town.

"Everybody knows me. I can do errands for you." I didn't add that I was bored. "Mike got his license a month ago. I can drive as good as Mike."

"You know that's so he can drive for his mother while his dad's going back and forth to Oregon," Dad said.

"Still, if Mike has a license, I can drive too, right?"

"Wrong," Mom said.

"But I already know how. I could take the truck down to Hawthorne to see Grandma Jean. I miss her."

"Grandma Jean wants us to visit. She said so," Lali said.

Mom smiled a little. "That's not the point."

"Mike's dad lets him drive their old Volvo." I tried one last time.

"You know that's different," Dad said.

So that finished my idea of driving to Hawthorne. Or to town, for that matter.

Mike came home from Hawaii, we started back to school, and then the doctors did another surgery on Ben, this time on his skull. They opened it up and put a plastic piece in where the bone had been. Mom drove to Palo Alto again and stayed at the Fisher House.

Saturday, Mike and I were skating in his driveway same as before Mom and Dad grounded me. His mom stuck her head out the door. "Cam, your grandfather's on the phone."

"Tell him you need to stay longer," Mike said. "We're just getting going."

I knocked the dirt off my feet, stepped onto their marble floor, and took the phone. "Hi, Grandpa," I said. I peeled off my jacket and tossed it on a chair.

"Cam, Lali and I are going down to Palo Alto to be with your mom. You need to come on home in time to fix your dad's dinner."

"What's wrong with Ben?" I asked.

"He's got a fever from the operation. They can't knock it down. I think he'll come through okay, but your mom is too worn out to be there by herself."

"He's bad, isn't he?"

"I don't know. You just come home for dinner. Your father needs family around too."

"I want to go to Palo Alto."

"Not this time. We won't be gone long. It's done then."
And he hung up.

My stomach clenched up like I'd been punched. I handed
Mrs. Gianni the phone and went to talk to Mike.

"I'm going home," I said. "Ben's really bad. They're going
to Palo Alto."

Mike shook his head. "What's up?"

"He's got a fever from the surgery," I said. "Grandpa and
Lali are going. Dad's not."

"Can't be that bad, then," Mike said. "Stay and we'll work
it off on the skateboards."

"No, I'm going." I jumped on my bike and took off.
I pedaled fast and could just see the ranch road in front
of me when Darrell passed in his pickup. He threw it in
reverse and lowered the window. "Hey, Cam, I'm going over
to get on a bull. Want to come?"

I looked toward my house. My muscles burned from
biking hard. I didn't want to think about Ben anymore. There
was still some time before dinner. "Yeah," I said, and I lifted
my bike and board into the back of his truck. I climbed in
next to him, and we turned toward the bull ring.

"Haven't seen you for a while," Darrell said.

"I've been around."

"You'll like this little Brahma we've got. He's one nasty
bull." He pulled the truck up next to the bull ring and we
got out. The arena smelled almost sweet. I listened to the
gravel under my tennis shoes. It sounded sweet too. We
climbed the platform and I breathed deep. My shoulders
relaxed. Right then, nothing mattered but getting on this
new bull. Andy Echevarria was fixing to ride. I leaned over

the holding pen to slap the bull into the chute. He mooed at me, and I heard tires crunching through the gravel. I turned and Mike's dad waved me over. Mike jumped out of the passenger side of the Volvo.

"We were on our way to your house but I saw you when we drove by." He handed me my jacket. "You left your coat."

"Thanks," I said.

"I thought you were going home."

"I was." I jumped off the platform, level with him.

Mike just looked at me. "We were skating."

"I had to go."

"Why would you leave and come over here when we can finally skate together?" he asked. And he stared some more.

"'Cause Ben might die," I said. "He's got an infection from the surgery. Don't you get it?"

"You're up next, O'Mara," Darrell called down to me.

"I get that you're going to ride a bull and your mom will take your skateboard again."

"Big deal," I said. When he didn't answer, I kept talking. "The trouble with you, Mike, is you never lost anything."

He narrowed his eyes and glared at me. "You better choose your friends. Now."

"I gotta go," I said. I climbed back up on the platform. I heard a car door slam. Mike had never been on a bull. He didn't get it. I lowered myself onto the tight little Brahma and pulled hard on Darrell's bull rope. What Mike didn't get was, starting right then, I didn't have to think.

Mike stopped talking to me at school. Everybody asked about it. "What's up with you two?"

"Nothing," I said. Nothing Mike couldn't fix by letting me do what I wanted. Bull ride. Skateboard. Whatever. I didn't need my friends telling me what to do. I had parents for that. Mike could rot. I had enough to fret about.

With Ben sick again, I skated alone at the Grange to let off steam. At night, I walked over to the Ruizes' and played video games with Favi. Dad scrubbed the kitchen till it shined. And then he did crossword puzzles. And we waited. This time Grandpa did the calling, and he said they had Ben on some "big gun" antibiotics. "The doctors say he'll pull through fine." I didn't trust it. My family had lied to me before, so I didn't feel any relieved.

After a few days, the phone rang, and it was Ben himself. He sounded good. "I'm sending Mom and Grandpa back to you pretty soon," he said.

"Great." I carried the phone with me out toward the barn. "I heard you were pretty bad off."

"Yeah, well, that's so. But they got the fever stopped." We shot the breeze for a while, and just before we hung up, Ben said, "Hey, remember that kid I saw in the hospital when you were here? The one who looked familiar? He showed up in my room to visit me after Mom left last night. He just came and sat down."

"Maybe it's the fever messing with your mind," I said. "What would that kid be doing coming to see you?"

"No, he was here. He didn't talk, though."

"Weird."

"Yeah, it was." He stopped. "Hey, the nurse is coming in with meds. I gotta go."

"Take care of your pretty new head," I said.

"Prettier than yours, bro'."

Now that sounded like Ben.

In February, they brought Ben home again, this time for a ten-day "visit." He was moving better and had a walker that the VA hospital had fixed up special so he could hang on to it with his artificial arm. He could use the walker to stand up and even take some steps. His speech was still pretty good, and his head looked almost normal after they patched him up. His hair was still growing in, but he didn't have to wear the dumb blue helmet anymore.

"Hey, Frankenstein," I said.

"Hey, dog face."

"Look at that, you're standing up. You decided to get off your butt?"

"Say *tush*," Lali said.

"Stop that," Mom said.

"Stop what?" Ben asked. The old Ben seemed to be coming back.

The days with Ben were good, but the nights were a different story. I slept upstairs and Ben slept down, but that first night, he screamed loud enough to wake us all no matter where we slept. I shot out of bed and skipped stairs on the way down. Mom and Dad tore downstairs right after me. Ben was sitting up in bed, eyes open, shrieking.

"Ben, wake up." Dad shook him. Ben took a swing at Dad

but missed him. "Ben," Dad yelled, "you're dreaming!" He shook him again, hard. Ben stopped screaming and looked at us blankly. You could see him trying to place where he was. "Ben, you're all right," Dad said quietly.

"I had a dream," Ben said. He was shaking. Mom turned on the light. Ben's face was ashy white.

"I'll get you some water," she said.

"I'm okay," he said. "I was dreaming. Bad stuff."

He sipped at the water and set the glass down next to his new hand on the piano bench. "They say I got more memory back along with my speech. It's bad. I can't sleep."

"Your dreams," she asked, "are they about the war?"

"It's like I'm still there," he said. "I can't stop them."

"Well, you're safe with us, you're home," Dad put his hand on Ben's shoulder.

"They were shooting at me. The noise. It wouldn't stop. All that fire." Then Ben saw me. He stopped talking and looked around, like he knew where he was. "Are you all up?" he asked.

"No, Grandpa Roy's deaf," I said. "And Lali sleeps through anything."

"What day's tomorrow?" Ben asked.

"Saturday."

"Stay up with me, Cam? We can watch a movie."

Mom and Dad kissed him good night and went back to bed. The TV reception was gone, except for the Kung Fu channel, since Dad had turned off the satellite service to save money. So, I rummaged through the DVDs and old videos. I put on *Top Gun*. Ben had always loved it, but as soon as the planes started firing, he got all sweaty. "I'll find something else," I said. "It's just a stupid movie." We settled on one of Lali's little kid movies about panda bears. I stayed with Ben till he fell asleep. The sun was lighting the sky behind the mountains when I got back to bed. I had chores to do, but they would wait. I closed my eyes.

The next day, Ben seemed fine. But I was worried. I called Grandma Jean.

"Cam, I'm glad to hear your voice."

"Me too. How are you?"

"How are *you*? I can tell—is something wrong?"

"Ben had this nightmare. It was awful. I don't know what to do."

Grandma Jean sighed. "Honey, you don't always have to be the one who fixes things. Let your parents and the doctors take care of it. They will."

"Are you sure? I wish you were here."

"I'll be there soon."

Just talking to her made Ben's dream seem less scary.

But that night, it happened all over again.

"They said this could happen," Mom whispered to me after Ben went back to sleep.

"Do you think he wakes up every night?" I asked.

"Oh, I hope not. It's the memories. He's got to sort out the awful memories."

"How long?" I asked.

"I don't know," Mom said. "I wish he were home for good."

"Let's give him something else to think about," I said. "Let Grandpa Roy and me take him to the bull ring. Let's do something he loves."

"In the morning. We'll talk in the morning." Then Mom went to bed, and I was so beat I lay back in the easy chair and slept next to my big brother.

CHAPTER TWENTY-ONE

I've got to be honest. For months Ben seeped into everything we did. "How's Ben doing?" everyone asked. They asked it at the feed store and at church, at school and at Grandpa's bingo night. Ben wasn't doing well. But we smiled and said, "As well as expected," or "Thanks, he's getting along."

So when we got pulled into Ben's nightmares and his remembering, there was only one thing I could think of doing that would take my mind and his right off his troubles. On a bull, you don't have time to think about anything. Mom wasn't so excited about me taking Ben to the bull ring, especially with the ice on the roads, but Grandpa and Dad got it right away. Grandpa called Tom Lehi, and Dad called Earl Wallace, Darrell's dad, and the Echevarria brothers—Andy's dad and uncle. Then they went a step further. They said they'd set up a chute in the Salt Lick corral. We'd all meet up there Sunday after church. Grandpa talked about laying a bonfire, and soon enough, the old guys were thinking about food.

"We're fixing to do a bull ride," I told Ben.

"Now?" he asked.

"Yeah, right now. Everyone's coming up Sunday. You can show off your new head."

Ben laughed. "It looks okay, huh?"

"You look good," I said. "The girls'll be hitting on you, for sure."

"Don't think so," he said. "They like guys who can walk."

"Don't talk like that, you dork," I said. "Sometimes you're just way dorky."

"Who you calling that?" he asked. And, you know, he threw his pillow at me.

We only had three days till Sunday, so Dad loaded some of those green portable railings into the pickup, and after school I helped him and Grandpa. We took the gas-powered auger, 'cause the ground was half-frozen, and some bags of cement. The corral at the salt lick was a loading area for putting the stock onto trucks. It had a V-shaped chute that ran into the corral for penning the cattle and another chute that ran out of the corral and up about four feet high for loading them onto a truck. Dad had added some extra height to the corral and doubled up the rails a couple of years ago when the government Bureau of Land Management, the BLM, wanted to use it for some wild horses, so it was stronger than your regular rail cow pen. But there wasn't any bucking chute. Dad was looking to fix that.

Now, we had a perfectly good bull arena in town with

solid sides and a real chute, but no one suggested we use it. I'm guessing they all understood—the salt lick was the center of our ranch. It was the center of us, really. It was where Lali'd learned to ride a horse and I'd roped my first calf. It was where Mom and Dad came to picnic when they were tired of the rest of us. Grandpa said it was the best place to break a green bronc, so he was figuring there'd be a little salt lick magic for bull riders, too. This was the place to cheer Ben up.

As luck would have it, the loading chute backed right to the gravel road, so Dad parked the truck next to the corral without having to venture into the mud alongside the fence. "I'm thinking we can block off a bucking chute in that one," he said, pointing to the broad chute that narrowed to the corral gate. "We can fix the gate to swing wide, and after the rides we can run 'em off into the loader."

"The steers are gonna fly right off the end of that ramp. A bovine bungee jump—is that what you're meaning to do?" Grandpa Roy asked, laughing.

"Not if we get Jones down here with the cattle truck. We'll have him back it up to the ramp and just load 'em in the trailer. And when we've got a few, we'll drive 'em back to the holding pen."

"The truck could bog down in the mud," Grandpa said.

"Then I'll bring up a load of gravel. Let's work on the gates."

Dad took to running the auger and Grandpa and I mixed cement. The rails were temporary, but there couldn't be anything half-baked about the posts. Not with bulls behind them. When Dad had a hole cut, we shoveled in some gravel from the road, set a metal pipe for a post, and I got the chore of shoveling in the concrete. It don't cure right in the cold, so after the posts were set, we piled on half bales of hay to keep the concrete from freezing. Then Grandpa wrapped it all in fence wire so the cows couldn't eat all our insulation.

We set posts for two gates—one to use for a bucking chute behind the corral gate and a second one behind that for good measure. The guys would strip the bull ropes off the bulls on the loading ramp before they shooed 'em into Jones's cattle truck.

"We'll hang the gates on Saturday and lay the bonfire," Dad said. "Ben'll love it."

Grandpa and I nodded. He surely would.

It was one fine party. The gates were ready, and Neil Jones hauled in the bulls. They came off the truck mooing, their flesh swaying under shaggy winter coats. Dad parked the truck and set Ben's wheelchair up right in the pickup bed. Ben had a front-row seat. Now that he had his skull repaired, he pulled on his cowboy hat and it fit just fine. Mom refused to watch the riding—it upset her too much. But she said she'd bring Lali, later, to the barbecue. Grandpa and Dad would be moving the bulls, and Andy Echevarria was bullfighting. Darrell and all the regular cowboys showed up to put on a show for Ben. The only one without a job or a bull rope was me. I was supposed to take care of Ben.

"It's a lousy break for you that you're not riding," Ben said.

"Uh-humh."

"So why don't you get out there and ride? I know you've been doing it."

"Well, Mom had a cow after I rode in Elko. I don't think she'll let me do it now," I said.

"I wouldn't count on that. Dad's the one out here, remember."

"Do you think?"

"Let's try something. Hey, Darrell," Ben yelled, "go see if Grandpa will put my bro' here on the lineup, will you?"

Darrell winked at me. "For you, Ben, sure." And before I could stop him, he jogged over to Grandpa and was talking and pointing my way. Then Grandpa talked to Dad, and they were all staring over at me. I figured to play dumb and nodded my head at them, business-like. Darrell came back looking like he'd eaten a canary. "You're in, squirt. Number seven. Lucky, right? Use my rope."

"No, he's using mine," Ben said. "Look in the truck, Cam."

So that's how I came to ride Hot Cakes on a freezing Sunday in February. He was a solid animal with two white spots on his rump, giving him his name. I'd practiced a piece since Grandpa'd seen me ride, and Dad, he'd never been around to see me on a bull at all. I was nervous. I pulled on Ben's glove and rubbed in some extra pine tar in case my shaking caused me to lose my grip. Hot Cakes looked as spooked as I felt. But with Dad and Ben and Grandpa waiting on me, I made myself get on him. He cocked his head back, like to ram me. I pulled the bull rope tight, pinched my hand closed, and signaled to let Hot Cakes fly.

His first landing jarred me hard and he spun like crazy.

It made me mad, and I spurred him. He let loose with his rear end, kicking, mule-style, up and out. That should have done me in, but I stuck for a couple more spins. Then I pitched off the side. The ground was rock hard—froze, I guess. It knocked the wind out of me. Hot Cakes took off in the other direction, and I made it over the fence. My dad shooed the bull right into the loading ramp, and I heard him clatter into the cattle truck.

The riders did three rounds apiece, and I had a good ride on a black mixed breed they called Sixty. That's for the number on his ear tag, which read sixty, I'm guessing. When we finished, they loaded all the cattle into the truck and started up the bonfire. Everybody was bragging on how good they rode and saying we'd have to come back to ride here again. Grandpa Roy was grinning like an old cat. More families started coming and set up barbecues for steaks and hot dogs and beans. The sun set and the winter chill came on fast. Grandpa Roy and Earl Wallace added wood to the fire.

We took Ben down off the truck, and I pushed him closer to the fire.

"Nice work today, bro'."

"Thanks," I said. "Do you ever wish it was you up there?"

"Well, yeah," Ben said.

I looked away, sorry that I'd asked.

Dad brought me a cup of coffee. "You can ride, son. It's good to see." Grandpa Roy nodded my way. I was dying to ask them. "So does Mom know?"

"Let's keep your mother from worrying about you,"

Grandpa Roy said. "Just don't go doing nothing stupid, and by the time she has time to think about you and bull riding, she'll be over it again."

"That's not what Grandma Jean says," I said.

"And that hasn't stopped you, I see," Dad said. I wasn't sure if he was mad about that or not. I'm guessing it was a draw, him being pleased with my riding and peeved that I'd gone against Mom.

Mom drove up with Lali and Favi. They helped themselves to the food and settled down with our family. The fire crackled and spit sparks. The old guys got to talking about back when this snowstorm almost did 'em in or when that BLM agent tried to overcharge them on their range fees. Then they started up talking about the salt lick.

"I gave salt to my horse and he learned to dance," Tom Lehi said.

"Yeah, I seen you waltzing with him," my dad said.

"Well, I put the salt in dinner the other night and my wife ain't slept since. We got the cleanest house in Humboldt County," Earl Wallace said.

"I tell you, that salt's magic," Grandpa Roy said. "Didn't you feel it when you rode tonight?" He leaned over to me and whispered so Mom wouldn't hear. "Seriously, Cam, it would behoove you to take some back home for your next bull ride." He winked at me. I couldn't tell if he was kidding.

Later, as folks began to pack up and start home, Ben said, "I wish it wasn't done."

"There's still plenty of food. And they'll be telling stories for a while," I said.

"My visit, I mean," Ben said. "I like it here."

"You'll be back home in Salt Lick before you know it." I leaned back on my elbows and looked into the fire. I squinted my eyes and the sparks blurred into bright streaks. "Just keep nailing it down there in rehab."

"When I'm done in rehab, I'm not fixing to come back here. I'm still a Marine," Ben said. "I'm hoping to be reassigned."

I sat right up. "You're what?" I knew he wanted to stay in the Marines. But didn't he know how scary that was? I wanted him to be happy—but didn't he care about Mom? Or Lali? Or me?

"Like I said, Cam, after I get new orders, I won't be home for a while."

TWENTY-TWO

Ben's brain was a mystery. He'd remember his locker combination from seventh grade but he couldn't add a column of figures. He named off all the men in his unit and pointed out streets on a map of where he'd been on patrol in Baghdad, but he got lost when the rehab folks took him on an outing to the grocery store. It was the little things he forgot—keys and numbers and whole clumps of words. But certain things were there, front and center, like he'd never been wounded at all. After seeing his nightmares, Mom spent more and more time with him in Palo Alto.

"Ben remembers the bulls," she said one night.

"What do you mean?" Dad asked.

"He can name every bull he ever made a time on. Look, they gave me a list." Mom handed a long list of bulls to my Dad. He mouthed the names to himself as he read them. "Amazing," he said. "Go figure that."

"He wouldn't forget," I said. "He wants to raise bulls. He knows the good ones."

"It's selective memory," Mom said. "They're trying to use it to help him remember other things. They say he might do better at home—because of the bulls and the ranch and all."

"Is Ben coming home? Tomorrow?" Lali asked.

"Not tomorrow, honey, but it could be soon." She turned to Dad. "They're evaluating his outpatient needs. If we can get him into Winnemucca for physical therapy and maybe down to Reno for some occupational training, then, yes, he could come home." She broke into a wide smile.

"Gotta fix a downstairs shower," Grandpa Roy said. "I can get the materials in the morning."

"There's no room in there, Dad," my dad said. "We'll have to bump out a wall."

"Gianni will help out," Grandpa said, and suddenly we went from feeling helpless and low with Ben in the hospital in California to a full-scale deal, building him a downstairs bedroom with a bathroom—sit-down shower, handrails, and all. "We'll lose some space in the living room, of course," Dad said, "but we can open up to the kitchen."

It was early March and the snow was still on the ground in the high country and spring calves were a month away, so when Grandpa said, "Gianni will help," it was a little short of the truth. When word got out that Dad and Grandpa and I were taking sledgehammers to our downstairs, two or three guys showed up every day to help out. Every one of them had an excuse. "Gotta get in shape and thought this was better than the gym, ha-ha." "Can't stand another day cooped up in my house." "I was driving by and thought you'd have the coffee on, and while I'm here, let me help you set that toilet." Friends came to help—like Darrell and Neil Jones—and so did folks you wouldn't expect to see, like Pastor Fellows. It was as if they were all just waiting for something, anything to do for Ben. Some days Mom just wept from the joy of it.

We had Ben's rooms set up by the end of the month, and the bill—well, nobody'd take any pay and the lumber and fixtures just showed up. Lali drew a sign for his door—Ben O'Mara, Super Hero—and she backed it with a multicolored page from one of her comic books. And best, when Ben was ready, Grandma Jean promised she'd come back too.

At the end of March, Ben came home for good. This time, when Dad called on the cell phone from the end of the ranch road, Grandpa, Lali, and I rode out on the ATVs to meet them. It was like all the fretting and anger from the last few months was gone. Ben was home. No more military forms spread out on the dining room table for Mom and Dad to fill in. No more Mom being gone for ten days at a time. No more wondering what Ben was up to and what I could do for him when he was so far away in the hospital. Ben was home. And now, I knew it, he'd only get better.

He had his new hand and some money the Marines gave him to pay for therapists since the VA hospital in Reno was too far to get to each week. He had his new room and Lali to bounce on his bed. He had Grandpa Roy to tease him, Dad to treat him like a man, and Mom to treat him like a kid.

I called Grandma Jean. "Ben's home. So when are you coming to see us?"

Grandma laughed. "Keep your shirt on. You know I'll get there soon as I can."

Lali leaned over my shoulder and called, "You promised," into the phone.

"And I'll be there. Let me talk to your mom about it. How's this weekend?"

But by the end of the first week, there was something wrong. And it was bad. The nightmares didn't come every night, but when they did, they were loud.

Darrell came by to visit after work. He brought Mom some tulips and a video of the Reno Rodeo to show Ben. "Take a look at this, Ben. This was right after you left." Darrell stopped. "Well, right before . . . " His face colored up. "You know . . . "

"Oh, stop," Ben snapped. "We all know what happened. I don't want to see that video anyway."

"Why?" Darrell asked.

"That was my life before. Before I was like this." Ben turned away.

Darrell couldn't get him to say anything else.

I tried to help out. "Ben, Darrell came up to see you. Talk to him, man."

Ben just turned his head farther toward the wall.

Darrell tossed the video on the table. "Call me when he's feeling better." And he left.

Darrell wasn't the only visitor, and Ben was rude to most

all of them. And when it was time to go to Winnemucca for therapy, he actually yelled at Mom.

"It's like the real Ben's not here," I told Mom. "It's like we got a different one—a mean one."

"Don't bother him," she said. "He's readjusting."

"I thought being home at the ranch was supposed to help."

"He needs more time."

"So is he just going to sit around and stew while his brain heals?" I asked.

"Cam, don't talk that way."

"We owe him," I said. "He's miserable."

"I think I know what we owe your brother, and he'll be fine. Don't bother him about it."

That's the deal. O'Maras don't talk about uncomfortable stuff, but I sure did feel I owed him something. I was the one who could walk and bull ride. I was the one who'd fouled up Dad's selling the fall calves—that could have taken care of some of the bills. I figured I owed everybody. Ben wasn't right. And, you know, I was sick of feeling helpless. And I was tired of being quiet.

I started the next day with Ben. After school I ran in from the bus and grabbed a pop. Then I stuck my head in his room and said, "Ben, you up? Let's go out to the barn. Grandpa thinks that new pinto is ready to try a saddle. I'm going to set one on him and see how he takes to it."

"Not now, I'm tired," Ben said. He sat in his wheelchair, staring out the window.

"You know you love seeing a horse broke to his first saddle. You can hold his head while I ease it on."

"Not now." Ben sounded grumpy.

But instead of backing off, I went in, took hold of his wheelchair, and threw a blanket over him. If Grandpa Roy could do it, I could too. "We're going to the barn," I said.

"Leave me alone, will you?" He threw the blanket off, but I pushed right over it.

It was bright outside and the sun warmed you just enough to feel like winter might go on back to where it came from. I bumped his wheelchair across the dirt and out to the barn. I pushed him inside the barn door and called to the pinto in the corral. He was friendly and came right over for some oats. It would be fun to saddle him. "You sure are nasty lately," I said to Ben. "And I don't know why. You can stand up. You'll be walking pretty soon, I know it."

"Maybe," he said.

I scratched the horse's nose. "So what's wrong?"

"What's wrong? Let me tell you. Start with this." He slammed his good hand hard on his wheelchair.

"No, what's really getting at you?" I insisted. "You aren't like you used to be. You were better when you couldn't even talk good—at least you were fighting then."

"Thanks for the info."

"Well, I'm tired of it. I want my real brother back." I knew I was being mean. "I'm tired of pretending you're doing so great and all. You're nasty half the time, and the other half you just stare. I'm sick of it."

"Forget you!" he yelled, grabbing at the wheel of his chair.

"No, *you*. Forget YOU." I stopped him from pushing himself toward the door. "Just tell me. What is it with you?"

That's when he started. He cussed and waved his

plastic arm at me. "What is it with me? You want to know?
I can't do anything. You want me to hold that colt while
you saddle him. How? What if he takes off? I can't walk,
I can't ride. I can't remember half of what anybody says.
For all I know, you told me this same garbage yesterday."
He banged around like he wanted to get up and chase
after me. "Look at me, Cam. Look good. You sit around
like me and see how it feels. You're the man now, Cam.
Right? You can go out skating and bull riding. Nothing
happened to you."

I glared at him. "Mom won't let me bull ride."

"But you do. I see you going off to practice with Darrell.
We were going to—"

"Yeah, I sneak around—and that's because of you. If you
weren't shot up and pitiful, Mom would lay off of me."

"Shut up, Cam." He stared at me. "They put me out,
you know. I could have gone back to my unit, to a desk
at least, but I can't remember nothing. Nothing normal,
anyway. I'm a Marine—and a bull rider—till they kicked
me out. And now what am I? A babysitter for Lali? Tell
me, Cam. What am I?" Then he put his head against the
stall, sniffed a couple of times, and let go and bawled.

"Oh man, listen, I didn't mean it, Ben," I said. "I didn't
mean any of it." I reached toward him but my feet didn't
move. He kept crying. It was the stupid TBI. I kicked the
wall. "You gotta stop that. I didn't mean it. I just want you
to fight the way you did before. I thought when you came
home, things would get better."

"Well, you were wrong," he said, sniffling.

"I was wrong to say that stuff. Geez, this is bad. Ben,

I'm so sorry. But I have to do something for you. What am I supposed to do?"

He didn't answer me, didn't even look up, really.

"You gotta fight, Ben," I was begging. "Things will work out. You can do anything if you try. You just have to believe it."

"*You* believe it. I don't believe in anything anymore."

My skin went cold and I could feel the blood draining out of my head. "You don't mean that. You can get better."

"Yeah, I can get better like you can ride that bull Ugly they're all talking about. It's just as likely."

"Well, I'd fight to ride Ugly at least. You're just a quitter."

Ben's face got red and now he really did try to get out of his chair. "Shut up. You go ahead and ride Ugly. Then I'll believe your garbage about doing anything. Then I'll do whatever stupid therapy they dream up."

"Okay," I said. "Just watch me, I will."

I turned the pinto colt loose in the corral, without bothering to try to saddle him, and slammed the metal gate behind him. When I came back in the barn Ben was quiet. I pushed him to his room. He sat staring at the blank TV. "I'm holding you to it, you know," I said, and I closed the door.

✳ CHAPTER ✳

TWENTY-THREE

I'd hardly talked to Mike since January, when he got mad with me for leaving his house to ride a bull. But now he was the only one I wanted to talk to. I took my bike and my skateboard, fixing to go down to see him. On the way through town I saw Darrell's truck outside the feed store. I pulled in. "Hey, Darrell, you got time to come by and see Ben again?" I asked.

"How's he holding up?" Darrell asked.

"He could use some company," I said.

"You know, I'm working full-time now and putting in hours training to ride Ugly. I'll come up if I can, but it might be a while."

"He's not always so nasty," I said, but I wasn't so sure anymore.

"Can't blame him, really." Darrell threw a fifty-pound bag of dog food into his truck. "But I don't have a lot of time. You say hi for me."

I wondered, with the way Ben was, who else would get too busy to see him. I bought a cookie from the pile at the front counter and rode up to Mike's. The dogs barked at me as I turned into the driveway. Mike must have heard it, 'cause he came out on the front porch. Favi was right behind him.

"Hey, Mike," I said. I jumped off my bike and let it fall to the ground.

"So?" he muttered.

I held up my skateboard. "I thought we could board."

"Why now?" he asked without moving.

"Come on, get over it. We're boarders," I said. I took my board around the driveway once and said, "Can you do this?" I ollied onto the rail. It's a game we played to mess with other kids at the skate parks. "Try this," we'd say, and jump into a 360, kicking the board around full circle and landing it. Most of the time, the guys would laugh and peel off down into the pool or up a ramp. Sometimes we'd get a taker. "No, do this," the kid would say, and he'd hit a ramp, ollie with his board right under him, land, and pivot grind off the other way. Then we had a game.

Now I started with Mike. "Come on, man, let's see you do it." I landed a 360 and then I missed an easy kickflip.

"What's up with that?" Mike asked. "Lali could do better."

"Thanks," I said. "Come on. Let's skate."

"You didn't come around before," Mike said, folding his arms tight across his chest.

I coasted up to the porch and kicked my foot down to

stop. "It's hard. I need you, man. Ben's driving me nuts."

"And I care?" he asked.

"Of course you care," Favi answered him. "You two are acting like two-year-olds. Cam's apologizing." She looked at me and raised her eyebrows. "Right?"

I sat on my board and grabbed the ends with my hands. My knees poked up by my chin. "Yeah, maybe," I said.

Mike parked himself on the top step and leaned back on his elbows. "So, what's with Ben? He's home. That's good, right?"

"No, it's weird. It's like we thought it would fix everything and instead it's worse. He's given up."

"You can see why," Mike said. "That's one ugly hit he took."

"Well, ugly or not, he's got to walk and remember stuff and get back to himself. He just sits."

"But your grandpa doesn't put up with that, does he?" Favi said.

"It doesn't matter," I said. "This is worse than before. All the teasing and messing around doesn't get through. Ben says he's useless."

I moved up on the porch and sat a step below Mike and Favi. A couple of little purple flowers had popped through the dirt, but mostly, everything was still bare against the mouse-colored ground. "So what are you going to do?" Favi asked.

"He says it's impossible to get better. He says it's about as likely as me riding Ugly."

"Well, *that* isn't about to happen," Mike said.

"I have to make it happen," I said. "I made Ben a bet—I'll ride Ugly. That will prove anything is possible."

"You bet him you'd ride Ugly?" Favi covered her face with her hands. Then she spread her fingers open and peered at me. "What were you thinking, Cam?"

"I got nothing to lose," I said.

"Except your brains. What about when that bull smashes you into little pieces?"

She was right, of course. That bull could kill me. Mom and Dad could disown me. I could fall off the dang bull and embarrass myself and prove Ben right all at the same moment. But there wasn't any choice, as I saw it. "Somebody's got to do something for Ben. I figure it's gonna be me. I can't stand watching him. I want my brother back."

"If you rode Ugly, you could use all that prize money to pay your family's bills," Mike said. "Or get Ben started with an AI breeding business like Amy Jones's."

"That's an idea," I said. Maybe Ben really could do that. He knew all the bulls—who they were and what their stats were. He could totally play that market, buy the best straws, put 'em away till the bull was real important, then sell those little vials for more money still—sell the right to the bull's offspring. Ben could so do that. And he always wanted to raise bucking bulls.

"Well, you better think a minute before you go planning how to spend all that prize money," Favi said. "You need a plan B. You know you're too young to enter to ride Ugly, don't you?"

"That didn't stop me in Elko," I said.

"Elko didn't have a fifteen thousand dollar purse," she

said. "They'll check stuff like that at this Ugly Challenge. It's not some small-town bull practice where they let you ride because they know your grandpa."

"How old do you suppose I have to be?" I asked.

"Eighteen," Favi said. "That's when you can sign your own life away. Or maybe if you were already sixteen, your mom or dad could do it for you. They make you sign legal papers when you ride in big competitions."

I said, "I'll ride him in Redding. There's a challenge there. I looked it up on the Internet. No one will know me or how old I am."

"Like you look eighteen," Mike said.

"I'm big. They always take me for a senior down in Winnemucca. And that's why I'm going to California. You'll see. I'm going to ride in Redding."

"They check ID in California, too." Mike shook his head. "They're gonna ask for your driver's license or birth certificate or something."

I crushed a clod of dirt under my heel. "Then I'll get a fake one. A false ID."

"Oh, please. That's illegal. Forget it." Favi rolled her eyes. "Your folks will take care of Ben."

"Right," I said. The problem with working your thoughts out on a skateboard, or the back of a bull, or pitching oranges is that you never just plain say what's on your mind. Now, these guys didn't get me, and I wasn't fixing to explain. "I'm getting an ID," I said. "You know anybody can help me out?"

Mike thought a minute. "I guess I know of a guy."

"I knew it," I said. "I knew you could fix me up."

"Don't thank me yet for any favors," Mike said.

"Cam, don't get yourself in trouble," Favi said.

I smiled at her. "It'll be okay. Just picture me riding Ugly. I'll make it happen. You'll see."

"Yeah, right," Mike moaned. "You're nuts, O'Mara. No way this is turning out good."

TWENTY-FOUR

That night, the three of us made the plan. I asked Mom if I could go into Reno on Saturday with Mike to see the monster trucks. I hated 'em really, but Mike liked the show and there really was one going on over there. Mom said yes, and I had my excuse to go into Reno. I emptied out my stash of birthday money and the pay I got last summer for mowing lawns, and had $150 in my pocket. I hoped that would buy Mike and me the monster truck tickets—we had to see the show or we'd get caught for sure—and leave enough to pay off the guy Mike knew who was going to take my picture and make my ID.

We left early in the morning. Mr. Gianni drove us to Reno. Mike practiced making rude sounds with air under his armpits, and I kept yawning and finally I tried to sleep. Mike's dad planned to do errands while we watched the truck show. What he didn't know was that Mike had his guy lined up to meet us on the backside of the Livestock Events

Center after we bought our tickets and went in.

We got to Reno by ten o'clock. My family didn't go to Reno too often except to Christmas shop or sometimes to take Grandpa Roy to get some medical tests. It's sure bigger than Winnemucca, and downtown has some places my mom didn't like me or Lali to see. You can spot 'em easy enough. They're painted pink or purple and the windows are painted over. In between are tattoo parlors and pawn shops. I pictured exactly where this ID guy had to live and figured I'd be staring down some bald-headed guy with dragons tattooed on his arms. Or maybe the "guy" would be a dried-up woman with red hair and a stale cigarette waiting to ask in a raspy voice if anyone had followed me. Honestly, I kind of liked the idea. My adrenaline was pumping.

Mike's dad dropped us off, and we promised to call his cell phone as soon as we were done. We bought the tickets, making sure we got our hands stamped so we could get back in later to meet Mike's dad. We pushed through the crowds, right out the back door, and past the row of blue outdoor toilets to the Dumpsters.

"Nice meeting place," I said.

Pretty soon, a clean-cut guy pulled up in a Toyota with a fresh wax job. He had on a University of Nevada sweatshirt and khaki pants. He rolled down the window and gave Mike a high five. "What's up?" he said, and pointing to me, "Is this the guy?" He laughed. "I can see why you need an ID. No introductions necessary. Let's see the cash. Two hundred dollars will get you a first-class license. Adult."

"I only need to be eighteen, so that's cheaper, right?"

He laughed. "Wrong. How much do you have?"

"Ninety bucks." Now he laughed louder. He motioned for me to come closer. I leaned in and he took my baseball cap off my head.

"Gianni, this kid isn't any older than you. He gets caught, I get caught. Come back when you're sixteen."

"I am sixteen," I said.

"Sure," he said. He turned on the motor and backed away from us. "Come see me in a couple years."

He drove away and we were left standing between the Dumpsters at the event center. "Great," I said. "That's your guy? Now what?"

Mike shrugged. "Want to see the monster trucks?"

Lali met me at the door when I got home. "How were the trucks? Did they jump over cars like they do on TV? Did you bring me anything?"

I handed her a stick of gum and tried to duck into my room, but Grandma Jean stopped me. "Good, Cam, you're home. Did you have fun?" and before I could answer her, she said, "Your mom needs help tilling the garden. I told her to wait for you, but she's already started. She's set on getting the onion starts in today. There's still a little daylight to work."

I didn't care about onion starts but Mom did. The ground was ready and today was the day she was planting 'em. "Let me change my clothes," I said. I took over with the rototiller and turned the dark, soft earth while Mom buried the little onions thumb deep. All the while I was thinking about my next idea for getting an ID. We worked until it got dark.

Finally, there was time to call Favi. "Did you get it?" she asked.

"No, the guy flaked. He said I was too young."

"You'll think of something to cheer up Ben," she said. "You don't have to ride Ugly."

"It's not just cheering him up. It's more. I'm going to ride that bull. Listen, I'm coming down to your house. Get out your art stuff."

I rummaged around in my bottom dresser drawer through all my crazy stuff I keep 'cause I like it. I found my rock from Lone Mountain with the fossils in it and the old comic books I'd gotten from Ben when I was ten. I moved the little straw duck decoy Grandma Jean made for me and finally found a plastic bag full of photos. I dumped them on my bed and pushed them around looking for the right one. Of course, it was under everything else. But I still had it. It was one of those strings of photos you get in the booth at the fair or in a cheesy store. Mike, Favi, and I had squeezed in together last spring and there were six pictures of us making faces. Mike did the lizard face and Favi could always look silly. When the machine had spit out the photos, we'd joked around about how one shot of me looked like a mug shot—or something that belonged on a driver's license. Now I cut it off and stuck it in my pocket. I went into Mom's office. It had taken some doing, but I'd got Mike to loan me his new driver's license—just till tomorrow. I put some photo paper in the computer and scanned the license. I hit print and waited for the copy.

I walked over to Favi's, knocked once, and went in.

"So, what are you thinking?" Favi asked.

I looked around. It was just us. "Look, I brought a copy of Mike's license and this photo." I laid them on the table. "We can paste something up and maybe we can use contact paper or go to the copy store and get it laminated," I said.

Favi looked at me like I was crazy. "That says 'Michael Enzo Gianni.' You can't use that."

"Enzo? Is that his middle name?"

"Cam, think, will you? It's got the wrong name on it."

"So we can paste something over it that says 'Cameron O'Mara.'" I put my picture on top of Mike's.

"Oh, please," Favi said. "You couldn't fool anyone with that."

"I could try."

She burst out laughing.

"Don't," I said. I clenched my fists and dug my nails into my palms. But then I took another look at me staring like a zombie from the copy of Mike's license. I couldn't stop myself from laughing too.

"Maybe you can get your mom to sign for you. Maybe then they'll let you ride," Favi said.

"Who are you kidding? She doesn't know I'm riding at all."

"Your dad, then?"

I thought about that, but no, Dad wouldn't go against my mother. "Maybe I can sign up online, and they won't need anything yet. Then I can think of something later."

Favi searched "Ugly Challenge" and we found the announcement, and sure enough, there was a registration form. "I'll type it in," Favi said. "Name?"

"Cam O'Mara."

"Address?"

"Route 7, Salt Lick, Nevada."

"Age?"

"What do I say?" I asked.

"Eighteen," she typed in. Then she stopped. "Cam, what if they put this in a database or something. What if next time you go to do something, they think you really are eighteen?"

"So?" I said. And then I picked up Mike's license and looked it over. "I guess I might want to try the bull riding circuit for real when I *am* eighteen. . . ."

"It's a fake age," she said. "Think of a fake name."

I didn't need to think, it just came out of my mouth. "Adam Carl. Start over and put in my cousin's name, Adam Carl."

That's when I became my cousin, Adam, who'd be nineteen now, just two months older than Ben. That is, if he hadn't drowned in Walker Lake on his birthday. Grandma Jean called him our guardian angel, and right now I could actually use him. It felt pretty good to bring him back to life. I knew his birthday, too, June 3, and so we were set.

Favi typed, "Adam Carl, PO Box 123, Hawthorne, Nevada. Age nineteen."

The day I rode Ugly, it wouldn't be me, it would be Adam, who grew up tall and strong but so baby-faced he could pass for fourteen. Or that's what I'd say if they asked about my age.

TWENTY-FIVE

They set the Ugly Challenge in Redding for mid-April. You wouldn't think it would make a whoop of difference when it was, but April is the middle of our spring calving, and that meant spending every weekend on the ranch. We brought the cows in close and watched out for when they dropped their little ones. Every day, there was a new bunch—from one part of the ranch or another—to round up, bring to the corrals, tag, doctor, and brand. It took one guy to flip and tie 'em, one to handle the vaccines and ear tags, and one with the Circle M O'Mara brand. If we found cows from another ranch, someone cut them out and penned 'em in a separate corral. And if Joneses or Echevarrias or Wallaces found O'Mara cattle, somebody'd ride over to bring 'em back. Nothing was as fun all year, and nothing took more time. If we had enough calves, Grandpa even put a crew together for Sunday. I had to figure some special plan to get me out of a day of calving and on the road to Redding.

First problem—I didn't have a driver's license or a car, so I figured I'd use the money I'd saved by not buying the ID and get a bus from Winnemucca to Redding. Now I just needed the reason to take all day Saturday and all of Saturday night to be gone. Easy, right?

Maybe not. I signed up for the first challenge on the Internet, and I was praying they didn't want me to show 'em my ID when I got there. Maybe if I cut the timing close they wouldn't bother to ask questions. But the bull riding started at six o'clock. I didn't know how many crazy cowboys would show or what the draw for order would be, so I had to be at the bull ring by five thirty, latest. "The bus might be late," Favi said. That meant taking the early one—so, I needed to be on the road at nine o'clock in the morning.

I complained over lunch in the cafeteria, "Grandpa Roy will never let me out of calving that early."

"Pretend you're sick," Mike said.

"Don't matter," I said. "'You can brand with a fever or you can brand without,' that's what he'll say."

"So go ahead and tell him what you're doing," Mike suggested.

That was some idea. "Tell him I'm lying about my name and my age and I'm going to Redding to ride a bull? I don't think so."

Favi sighed. "Use your head, Cam. Your *mom* will let you go. Tell her we're having a study group—all day. You can say we're all going down to Winnemucca to use the library. I'll ask my mom to drive us. When she leaves, you can go to the bus station." I had to give her credit. Favi could think on her feet.

"Okay. See, I knew we'd figure it out," I said. "High five, Favi!" We had a plan. A good one. "But what about when I don't come home?"

"I can tell my mom you went home with Mike," Favi said.

"And by the time your folks find out, you'll already be gone," Mike said, grinning.

The plan would have worked too, except Grandpa Roy heard me talking to Mom in the kitchen and he was none too happy. "You can't take all day, even if you are studying," he said.

"Of course he can," Mom said. "His grades are important. He'll help on Sunday." Not that I'd be awake on Sunday morning after spending all night riding home on the bus, but as long as I wasn't handling the hot branding iron or the ear-notch knife, I figured I wouldn't be too dangerous. And if I came home with fifteen thousand dollars and a kick in the pants for Ben 'cause I'd won our bet, well, they might just decide to let me sleep in.

"You can get in some time at the corral before Favi's mom picks you up. Tell her to meet you at the house at nine thirty. That way, we can start at six when the sun's up and you'll get in three hours."

"Nine thirty's late," I said.

Mom laughed. "Since when have you worried about missing a half hour of library research? That sounds good to me, Roy."

So there I was, with half an hour to shave off the time I

needed to get to the bus station already. Maybe this wouldn't work. But I peeked into Ben's room as I left the kitchen and he was napping *again*. Yeah, I was ready to try it.

Saturday morning started out well enough. Men get a rhythm going, working the calves, and since I was leaving early, that made me the pick-up man. Pick up the ropes. Pick up the coffee. Pick up the stray O'Mara calves over at Jones's and herd 'em back. I had enough time to do it too, and I was happy to get the ride on Pepper.

I didn't go out to the corral where they were working on the calves but rode directly to Jones's ranch to fetch three of our calves and their mothers that they'd brought in on their roundup. They were waiting for me in a little pen behind the big barn. I waved at Neil Jones, opened the gate, and shooed the cows ahead of me. I swung my rope, and they started down the road. It's mornings like that when you could take me for a real cowboy. The cattle were moving good, and my adrenaline was already kicking in. I got a rush from thinking about my plan and another one from thinking about Ugly. That got my heart pumping more.

I was feeling good, riding along and watching some quail rustle around in a mahogany bush that was about to bloom. Then I glanced up at the cows. Three cows. Two calves. That wasn't right. Now, I could lose a mom and her baby, and it would make me mad, but we'd find them sooner or later. But you can't just lose a calf. They need their moms, and there's coyotes and mountain lions and stuff that will take down a lone calf. I pulled up my horse and scanned the desert. The little group I was herding got to grazing and picking at the ground. The cow missed her baby and started calling in long, sad wails. She'd wander off too if I didn't keep them moving. I had to choose. And it wasn't really a choice. I whistled and hurried the cattle toward our own corral. Grandpa met me at the gate.

"Get 'em all?" he asked.

"One of the calves took off halfway between Joneses' and here. I couldn't see him. I brought these on over and figure I'll go back for the calf."

"Okay," Grandpa said. He handed me a thermos of coffee and closed the gate on the five animals I'd collected.

I rode back at a fast lope and started making circles from where I'd first missed the calf. I checked for tracks, but the ground was hard and I wasn't finding any. The sun got higher and I knew it was getting late. I had to go. I'd ask Dad to come back on the ATV. I started riding toward our corral and just then, I heard a bawl. It started low and went high and long. It was a calf calling for its mom. I turned Pepper toward the sound. She stepped carefully down a slope and into a dry wash. The calf was still mooing. The little guy was getting pretty worked up from the sound of him. "Keep calling," I said. "Just keep calling."

I spotted him at the bottom of a second slope that was covered in talus—slippery little rocks that bust off the mountains from freezing and thawing. Walking down talus is like trying to keep your footing on ball bearings. The calf had slipped down and was wedged between a boulder and a piñon pine that was growing out from under it. "You got yourself in a fix, didn't you?" I said. I stopped Pepper at the top of the slope. I tied my rope to her saddle horn, grabbed it, and slid down the hill on my butt, letting the rope unwind as I went. The rocks showered out in all directions. "No wonder you got stuck." I dug my heels in as I got close to the bottom and coughed from the dust I stirred up. The calf was scared to death, bawling and pawing at the rocks, trying to get a grip. "You're a cute one," I told him. I looped the rope over his neck. Then I got behind the calf and pushed. He yelled some more, but with me lifting his tail end, he got some traction on the front and moved out. He ran straight down the wash. The rope pulled taut and jerked him back.

Pepper's a good cow horse. She held him tight. "So now we have to get you back there," I said, pointing to the top of the slope. I crawled up on my hands and knees. The rocks scratched my palms and dug into my shins. At the top, I pulled myself onto my horse and walked her backwards. She worked the rope hard. With each step she took, the calf climbed closer to the top. He lost his footing a couple of times, but Pepper didn't let him slip. She'd sidestep and pull harder. Slowly, the little guy made his way up the hill.

"You're a troublemaker," I told him. He looked at me like nothing had happened. His eyes were big and soft against his cinnamon-colored face. "That took some doing. Now let's get you back." I pulled in the rope and led him toward our branding corral. The sun heated my back. I stopped to judge its height and it was well above the mountains. I'd forgotten how late it was getting. Maybe too late already. I kicked my horse and tugged on the calf's rope. Pepper took off at a lope, and the calf barely kept up. Still, it seemed like it took forever to cover any ground. Finally, we saw our corral.

I handed the calf off to Grandpa Roy and rode back to

the barn. Favi's car was in front of the house. She ran out to meet me. "Where have you been?"

"I had to bring in a calf. I'll cool Pepper off and we'll go."

"No, we won't," she said. "It's ten forty-five. The bus is gone and you'll have to take a jet to get to Redding if you leave now."

It took a minute to sink in. "We can't get there," I said to myself.

"No," Favi answered. "My mom's waiting."

There was no getting out of that part of the plan. Favi and I spent the day writing history reports at the Winnemucca library. And, I imagined, Darrell was on his way to Redding to ride Ugly and win my prize money.

TWENTY-SIX

Okay, I'll say right off—I couldn't wait to hear if he'd won. I called Darrell's cell phone late on Saturday night. Now, he might have thought I was cheering him on, but I was dying to know if the prize money was still on the table.

"So, did you ride Ugly?" I asked.

"Well, I sat on him," Darrell said. "That's one bad bull. I sat on him and then he just shot me over his shoulder to the left. He's a left-hander, but the dang beast did an about-face. I've got the feel of him now, though. I'll give it a good go next time."

"Next time?" I asked. "When's next time?"

"Well, that's the good part. If nobody rides him in Bakersfield next week, they're bringing him on over to Winnemucca."

"Winnemucca? Are you gonna try in Winnemucca?"

"Darn right, unless some fool sits eight seconds in

Bakersfield. They're only doing three more challenges, then they're shipping him out on the pro circuit."

"Where's the last one?" I asked. Bakersfield was too far away, and I figured I'd have to have a hole clean through my head to try to pass myself off as Adam Carl and ride Ugly in Winnemucca. Everybody'd know me there.

"Colorado, down near Grand Junction. That's in June, but don't count on seeing him there. I'm riding him right here at home first."

"Sure you are," I said. "Well, sorry you didn't win."

"Me too," he said. "But this way you can watch me ride." The connection turned to static. "You're cutting out. I'm . . . "

Well, that about did it. There'd be no way I could ride Ugly now. I'd have to think of something else, or maybe Ben would just get better. And maybe the spring calves would bring a good price and things would look up all around. But who was I kidding? Ben was as depressed as he'd been since they let him out of the Marines and sent him home. Dad was selling more calves than we should part with, and Mom was stressing more every day from watching Ben turn sour. And without rubbing Ben's nose in the idea of doing the impossible, without riding Ugly, I couldn't do anything about it.

I didn't want to get out of bed on Sunday, but I had to. When I got to the corral, Grandpa Roy handed me the branding iron. "Mark 'em careful," he said. "That's our O'Mara name on there." They'd brought in a big load of cows and calves from up Sugar Peak, and I set to heating the iron and etching our brand into the new calves' behinds. It was hard to stay mad out there with the babies bawling and jogging off to their mamas. They were just so cute. And as I set that brand on the calves, one after another, it came to me. Ben and I, we were as good as branded too. O'Mara's. We were the same. No wonder Ben was depressed. This was our life: working the ranch, stringing barbed wire, riding bulls. What did he have left to look forward to?

And then, while the iron sizzled on a little caramel-colored heifer, Ruiz asked Grandpa, "Do you want me to run this bunch back up Sugar Peak? I'm not sure if the range will hold out after this winter. Maybe keep them at the salt lick?" And Grandpa answered what I'd heard him say a thousand times. You could call it O'Mara family rule number one. "Do what you think is right."

As I pulled the iron off the calf and Dad unwound the rope holding his feet, I knew what was right. I had to do something for Ben. If I couldn't ride in Redding or Bakersfield, maybe I'd get myself to Grand Junction in June somehow. And if Grand Junction was too far, then there was only one place left to ride. . . .

Yeah, I had a hole in my head to ride in Winnemucca, but then, Ben had one too, so I guess we matched. At first, I figured I'd aim for Grand Junction, but it was even farther away than Bakersfield, and the more I thought about it, the more I worried that somebody'd ride Ugly first. The worst was knowing Darrell was giving it another try. And in Winnemucca, maybe Andrew or Favi's uncle would throw in too. One of them could ride him before I got my chance.

Grand Junction was too much of a long shot. I didn't like it, but I was getting a clear picture.

That evening I talked to Favi while we raced cars on one of her video games.

"I'm riding Ugly at the next challenge," I told her.

"Where?" she asked.

"Here. In Winnemucca. They're bringing him over at the end of April."

"You're crazy," she said. She spun her car around a corner on the virtual racetrack. "How are you going to ride a bull in Winnemucca? Your mom will find out."

"She'll find out anyway," I said. "And Grandpa and Dad already let me ride up at the salt lick."

"Well, how are you going to pass for your dead cousin when everybody in the stands knows you?"

She had me there. I watched as she ran her car off the track and crashed. "I don't know. You figure it out." I started up my car—a Ferrari—only the best for my race car.

"Listen, Cam, this isn't like skipping your algebra homework. I'm sure this whole thing is illegal."

I ran my car up to 180 miles an hour and accelerated into a turn. There were barrels on the right, and I turned hard left not to smash into them. "You're right," I said. "You forget I thought of it." My car spun out and slammed into a concrete wall. The screen flashed, "You Lose."

"You know," Favi said softly, "Ben can do correspondence classes. He can learn accounting like your mom or start an Internet business or something."

I shook my head. "Like, can you really see Ben as an accountant? And he won't try anyway. That's why I have to win our bet."

Favi started her car. She was way too careful on the straightaway. She'd never beat me if I could stay on the track. "Just don't do anything stupid," Favi whispered.

"Too late. I sent in the entry fee."

Favi's car flew right off the track. She put the controller down and stared at me. "Why'd you do that?"

I punched her shoulder. "Just come to the fairgrounds and watch me ride. And maybe you can keep my mom from killing me when she finds out. That's all I ask."

"That's all?" Favi said. "That's all? You know you'll be grounded till you graduate, and what if you *do* need an ID? You aren't Adam Carl. What if they catch you? You're certifiably crazy."

I started my Ferrari around the track. "Just be there, okay?" I glanced at her and my car crashed. "I need you."

Now I was the one marking off days on the calendar. I met with Darrell to help him train, I said, but I always got a chance to ride. I didn't worry about Mom finding out. I was way past that. I did all my homework and tried to think of extra chores to do. I taught Lali to tie her shoes—finally—and I planted more of the garden with Mom and Grandma Jean. The last thing I had a mind to do was make anybody mad or crazy with me. Except maybe Ben. He watched more TV every day, replaying the same old videos and kung fu movies. He didn't even read with Lali anymore.

And his walking was getting worse instead of better.

"Get up off your butt and do your exercises," I told him.

"You do 'em," he said.

"What about taking a correspondence course?" I asked him.

"Are you going to read the books for me?"

"Well, don't just sit around."

Ben glared at me. "Go away."

The only thing that perked him up was going to the bull ring. Grandpa and I took him when we could, but the ranch chores and my homework kept us busy, and I wasn't taking him when I practiced with Darrell. So there it was. Ben was sitting more and living less. It was like I was watching him shrink right down into himself, and I didn't know how to reach in and grab him back. I wished he was a calf and I could just rope him and push on his butt to get him moving. Instead, he about finished me off when he came into the kitchen one night, pushing his walker.

"You want some milk?" I asked him.

"Sure." He sat down and sipped at the milk. Some of it ran down his mouth on account of his right hand still wasn't as steady as you might like. The milk soaked into his T-shirt, and he swatted at it with his hook.

"I'll get that." I reached for a kitchen towel and wiped his shirt.

"Stop. It's okay," Ben said.

"Do you want a clean T-shirt?"

"Just milk. That's all I want." Ben took another drink. Nothing spilled.

"See. Now that's working for you. Good job."

"Good job?" Ben asked. "Come on, I'm just drinking stupid milk. Don't talk down to me, Cam."

"I wasn't. I don't think I was. . . . Do you want anything else? Grandma made cookies."

He turned his head away and whispered, "Cam, I'm only nineteen."

"So?" I asked.

"So, look at me. I can't even . . ." He set down his glass. Tears ran down his face. "Cam, who's gonna want me?"

After that, I hung more and more hope on my eight seconds with Ugly.

TWENTY-SEVEN

I got an envelope in the mail at the end of April. I grabbed it out of the pile from the PO box before anyone else saw it, and ran to the barn to open it. There it was, my number—thirteen—and my entry confirmation—*The Ugly Challenge: Adam Carl, Hawthorne, NV, age 19. Registration on Saturday, April 25, between 5 and 6 p.m. Good luck.*

Now, I didn't say anything to anyone. I just waited for Saturday. And when it came, I got up early, did my morning chores, and pretended to read the paper until Ben was watching cartoon videos with Lali. I went into his room and rustled around in his dresser until I found what I was looking for. I tucked his lucky socks into my pocket. Then I opened the closet and took out his bull rope, protective vest, and glove.

"Sorry, Ben," I said to the empty room. "I don't have any of my own gear yet."

I zipped everything into my gym bag with my boots and the entry forms and slipped outside to the truck. I threw the stuff in the back and checked for the keys. Grandpa always left them in the ignition, and today wasn't any different. Now, I'd already tried to buy a fake ID and lied to my mom all year, so I guessed taking our truck for the afternoon wouldn't be much worse. I had to sign in at five o'clock. I'd leave right at four so I could get there on time and maybe my folks wouldn't miss the truck in time to track me down before the bull riding was over.

I tried to keep busy the rest of the morning. I took Pepper out for a ride. I helped Dad trim some low branches off the cottonwoods that lined our driveway and used the chainsaw to cut them up. I went back to the house and Grandma Jean had lunch going.

"I'm not hungry," I told her, although my stomach was growling. I was afraid I wouldn't keep the food down. And I was afraid something I did or said would spill the beans.

"Spill the beans," I said out loud. Then I asked Grandma, "Where do you suppose that phrase comes from?"

"Let the cat out of the bag, that's what I'd say," Grandma said, flipping a quesadilla. "What're you thinking about?"

"Nothing," I said.

She gave me a long look that made me figure she knew more than she possibly could about my day. "Well, whatever you're up to, just remember if a frog had wings, he wouldn't bump his butt hopping."

"Rivet, rivet," Lali called from the other room. She

hopped right up to the stove. "Grandma, there's a carnival in Winnemucca today. Can we go?"

"Ask your mother, sweetie."

"You can't go," I snapped.

"Why not?" Lali demanded. "Mom, Mommy!" She ran off. I followed her to Mom's office.

"Mommy, I want to go to the carnival in Winnemucca and Cammy says I can't."

Mom hugged her. "Dad's taking you to your first T-ball practice today. Remember?"

"Can we do both? Cammy, come to T-ball with me."

Mom answered. "No, we can't do both. But you could go to her T-ball practice, Cam. That would be a nice thing to do."

"No thanks," I mumbled. "I've got plans." I hurried out before she could ask again.

About one thirty, I went in the new downstairs bathroom and threw up.

"Are you all right?" Mom called through the door.

"Yeah," I said.

"I'll get a thermometer," she said when I came out.

"I'm okay, I just ate something wrong."

"Well, what? You didn't eat lunch, and we all had the same breakfast. Are you catching the flu?"

"I had some cold pizza in my room," I lied.

"Cam, you can get really sick eating food that isn't refrigerated. And with summer coming, you'll draw ants upstairs. What possessed you to have pizza in your room?"

So there I was, two hours from "borrowing" my first car and probably ending life as I knew it, and I was lying about why I'd taken nonexistent pizza to my room and eaten it, when I couldn't have ate it at all 'cause it never existed in the first place. "I don't know. I like pizza, and I didn't want Grandpa to eat it," I said.

"Grandpa wouldn't eat your pizza. Where'd you get it?"

"From Mike."

"You boys have to use your heads," Mom said. "We should take your temp anyway." She went for the thermometer and I ducked out the back door. I saw dust down the ranch road coming toward the house. I watched the car come closer. It was Mike's dad's old Volvo. I walked out to meet him. Favi was in the car too. "What's up?" I asked.

"We came to take you to Winnemucca," Mike said.

I stared at Favi. "Why would I go to Winnemucca?"

"Oh, shut up," Mike said. "Favi told me, and we're going to be there if you need some protection from your mom."

"Or a ride to the emergency room," Favi added.

"I've got it covered," I said, thinking of my gear stowed in Grandpa Roy's truck.

"No, you don't. How are you getting there?" Favi asked. "Go tell your folks we're going to the movies and come on."

"I hadn't planned this. How will I get my cowboy hat? Why'd I need a cowboy hat at the movies?"

"You worry too much. Just go get your hat, ask your mom if you can go to the movies, and come on," Favi said. She scooted over to make room for me next to her in the front seat.

I went to the truck, pulled out my gym bag, and handed

it to her. "I'll be back." I did just what she said. I picked up my cowboy hat and while I was at it, I stuffed the good luck packet Grandma Jean made me into my jeans pocket. It wouldn't hurt to have a little O'Mara salt with me.

"Mom, Mike and I are going to the movies," I called.

"Not before I take your temperature."

"I'm feeling good now. Honest. I'm going to the movies, okay?"

"You're sure you're all right?" She felt my forehead with the back of her hand. "Well, you feel cool enough."

"Mike's waiting," I said.

She peeked out the window. "They're already here? Sure, have fun."

Grandpa Roy looked at me funny and asked, "You have money for that movie ticket?"

"No."

He handed me a twenty. "Don't spend it all in one place." He winked at me.

I ran outside before I lost my nerve and jumped in the car.

We drove down to the fairgrounds. It wasn't like fair day, with hundreds of cars pulling up to the parking lots. But there was a goodly amount going on with stock trucks, and the radio station had set up a tent. People pulled in to go to the cheesy carnival the Boys and Girls Club was holding for the occasion—the one Lali wasn't going to, thanks to T-ball. The Junior Rodeo was doing a mutton-busting demonstration before the Ugly Challenge, and all the moms and dads were hovering around with their five-year-olds in their boots and bicycle helmets, waiting for their ten seconds of fame.

"Whose idea was this?" I asked.

"Oh, can it," Mike said. "We've lived through this bull-riding stuff with you for months, and you're still set on making a fool out of yourself right here, so go do it. We'll keep an eye out for anybody you might know."

They dropped me by the south gate, and Favi gave me the gear bag and squeezed my hand. "Good luck," she said. "Do it for Ben."

"Thanks." I squeezed her hand back and turned toward the arena. I followed the string of people making their way toward the stands. Really, whose fool idea was this? I looked around and I didn't see anyone I knew. That was a blessing. And a surprise. I hoped Mike could do what he said and keep any Salt Lick folks away until I was signed in and ready to ride.

That was the first time I'd honestly thought about the ride that day, I'd been so fixed on how to get out of the house and down to the fairgrounds. Not that I hadn't pictured it in my head a thousand times. There was Ugly and there was me, sitting on him, knocking around but keeping my seat, riding, winning. But I hadn't pictured that today, and now that I was close enough to smell him, well, I broke out in a sweat. Maybe I should try a taste from the packet of lick salt in my jeans. I wiped the back of my neck and said out loud, "It's for Ben."

"What's for Ben?" a cowboy asked. He carried a bull rope

and wore a tall buckaroo-style hat. That made him local, and I figured he was my competition.

"My ride," I said.

"You mutton busting, kid?" he asked, laughing. "You're awfully big for that."

I turned my back and walked toward the table where the cowboys were signing up. I was almost in. All I had to do was sign my name and hope they didn't ask for any proof. That was the catch. A couple of cowboys were already filling out their insurance waivers. They left the table adjusting their numbers. I needed a bigger crowd. I waited till a guy came up with all his family—wife, four little kids, the whole deal. I crowded in right behind them.

"Name," the man said to me.

I looked up. "Adam Carl, sir," I said, cool as could be.

"Let's see your ID."

"I lost my wallet yesterday. Haven't had time to replace it," I said. I think my voice shook.

The man held my registration papers up and looked them over. "Too bad about your wallet," he said.

One of the cowboy's kids started crying and another one was whining to get a cotton candy. I shifted my weight to my other foot.

The man smiled again. "You don't look nineteen, son."

"It's the Indian in me." I smiled.

I wished the kid would throw a real fit and push this along, but instead he settled down and the family left. It was just me and this man. "Can I go on in?" I asked.

"Wait here," he said. "I have to check this out." He left

the table and climbed the bleachers to talk to a silver-haired man in a John Deere cap. This was not good. I thought about leaving. Then someone yelled, "Hey, Cam!" I turned before I thought to stop myself, and there was Darrell walking up behind me.

TWENTY-EIGHT

What are you doing here?" Darrell asked.

"I'm signing up to ride this Ugly bull, same as you," I said.

"Huh?"

"My cousin, Cam, told me about the challenge." I practically glued my eyes to his, hoping he'd get it—and quick before the official came back. "He said to come on up from Hawthorne. I'm signing in, see?" With that, I shoved my entry form in his face, pointing at the name and age.

"Huh?" he said again. Then he eyed me. "Adam Carl?"

"That's me. I'm just older than my cousin, Ben." I pushed the paperwork into my gym bag. He started to say something, and I had to stop him. "Ben's the reason I'm here," I said. "I heard my cousin could use a lift and maybe some of the prize money to get his life going again. You're friends with him, right?"

Darrell took in the two old guys who were still talking in the stands. "Right," he said. "But you aren't leaving with the prize money."

"Maybe, maybe not," I said.

Darrell spit out of the side of his mouth. "You're something else," he said. And the two of us waited for the officials at the table.

The man talked to me first. "Son, this looks a little fishy to us. I'm afraid you're going to have to have some proof of age."

"Like what?" I asked.

"Something that will convince us," the official said.

I looked at Darrell. He could get me kicked out or he could stand up for me and help me get in. He didn't do anything. It was like he'd never met me. I said, "I'll find something."

The little kids were lining up for the mutton busting, and a stream of folks came through the gate and climbed into the stands. I sat on the bottom bench and put my head in my hands. I didn't have anything to show them. Maybe Mike and Favi could tell the man I was Adam. I jogged to the gate where they were staking out the parking lot. "I'm sorry, Cam," Mike said. "Darrell just went right by and there's a bunch of guys from Salt Lick who came with him."

"Darrell's riding, what else would he do?" I said. "Come on, don't worry about watching the gate anymore. I need you guys to say you know me and that I'm Adam Carl."

"I'm not lying to the officials for you," Favi said.

"I'll do it," Mike said, glaring at Favi. He followed me back to the registration table.

"This is my friend, Mike Gianni," I said. "He knows who I am."

"This guy's Adam Carl. He's from Hawthorne and comes up this way to mess around with us," Mike said.

"So how old is he?" the official asked.

And that's when Grandma Jean trotted up, breathless, pushed in front of Mike, and set her rose-covered bag on the table with a thump. The man jumped back a piece and I froze. "He's nineteen if he's a day and I ought to know. That's my grandson you're bothering."

"Excuse me, ma'am?" the man said, staring at Grandma. She smoothed out her red knitted poncho.

"That's my grandson," she repeated. "Adam Carl. He lives with me down in Hawthorne. Do you want to see his baby pictures?" And just like that, she opened her bag and dumped it on the table. From the pile of rubber bands and candy bars, she picked out the little lavender photo holder she kept with Adam's pictures. I couldn't watch. She handed them to the man and said, "You can see the family likeness, I think. Some kids don't change from baby to adult." And then I looked down and sure enough, from those pictures, I could pass for little Adam if he'd actually grown up. "Now are you going to let my grandson ride this darned bull so we can see a real cowboy?" she asked.

The man shook his head. "Well, you do look young."

The silver-haired man said, "He looks big enough. The kid's probably nineteen." He turned to Grandma Jean. "How do we know those baby pictures are him?" That was a good question. I held my breath.

"Land, you are stubborn," she said. She opened the back

of her wallet, unfolded a piece of paper from it, and laid it in front of the official. "There. That's his birth certificate. I had it copied, just in case you wouldn't believe him. He doesn't look his age to some folks."

The man read it and looked at the pictures she'd spread on the table. "Sorry, ma'am, we have to be extra careful." Then he turned to me. "You're number thirteen, third to ride tonight. Get in the lineup."

I started to say something to Grandma Jean, like, "What are you doing carrying around Adam Carl's birth certificate?" but she shook her head at me and grabbed Mike's arm. She turned him toward the stands and marched him away.

I walked behind the chutes. The cowboys had a space set up for their gear in a big tack room. I spotted Darrell standing in the middle of piles of protective vests, helmets, hats, and some cowboys' lucky jeans. He had his back to me and was zipping up his vest. "Hey," I said, "thanks."

"Thanks for nothing," he said. "It's you that's gonna get yourself whooped tonight." The cowboy in the buckaroo hat turned and looked at me.

"That mutton buster's riding bulls?" he asked Darrell.

"He's actually pretty good at it," Darrell said.

"Well, they keep looking younger. I must be getting old," the guy said. He picked up his hat and left.

"Where is everybody?" I asked.

"They're out at the arena, or they rode earlier in the day. With fourteen riders signed up, they divided us up into groups. We're in the last bunch and ain't nobody rode him yet today. They had to stagger the rides or that poor bull would about wear out."

"Worn out sounds good," I said.

Darrell smiled. "Yeah, worn out or mad. And how did you get in here?"

"Don't ask," I said. "And call me Adam."

"Then tell me—how exactly is your riding this bull helping Ben?"

I zipped up Ben's vest and pulled the glove and pine tar out of my bag. "I made him a bet. Just like I did with you and the skateboarding. If I ride this bull, Ben has to get up in the morning and do something for himself. If I don't ride him, well, he'll just say there ain't no reason to hope for the impossible. And with the prize money, we're gonna set him up with a business he can do, give him something to wake up for."

Darrell looked at me. "That so? Well, you got to beat me first."

I knew that.

There were only four of us riding Ugly that night. Turns out the rest of the cowboys were there for the show—either team roping or riding the other bulls the stock men had brought over. And the kids had their mutton busting. They were spacing the four of us through the other events. I was number thirteen. Darrell was number fourteen. I had my shot before him, but it wouldn't matter much, since the way they'd laid this out, any of us that rode Ugly in the Winnemucca Challenge would split the prize.

I paced around the tack room and tried to pray. The Christian bull riders on TV, they always pointed skyward or knelt to give thanks when they came off a bull. It seemed like some good insurance to me, but I couldn't get the prayers going when I was so wound up. Everything seemed pretty dusty and down-here-on-earth to me.

I went outside. The sun was setting and the lights were on in the arena. The announcer called, "And now for our youngest cowboys and rodeo gals. Here they are, ready to rock and roll and ride, ride, ride on the meanest bunch of woolly sheep we could find in Humboldt County. Give a big hand to the little mutton busters."

I climbed the fence and looked around. Eight kids were lined up in their helmets. The oldest looked about seven. The announcer went on. "Here's a big cowboy, all of six years old, Taylor Graham." A dad opened the gate on the sheep pen and the kid shot out, arms wrapped around the sheep's neck. He rode till he slipped over to the side and lost his grip. He landed on the ground and started to cry. "That's a great ride for Taylor, let's give him a hand." He wiped his eyes and walked over to his parents. The second and third kids rode. So far, Taylor was the only one who lost it. I could so get how he felt. I wanted to cry and I wasn't even on the bull yet. They gave a big girl in blue cowboy boots the first-prize ribbon. She grinned like she'd won the lotto.

"Well, cowboy up, 'cause we're going to bull riding," the announcer said. "Our first sirloin jockey is Manny Rodriguez from Bend, Oregon. He'll be taking that challenge on Ugly. And what do you say, are you thinking it will be a cold day in August before our bull, Ugly, let's a cowboy stick eight seconds? Good luck, Manny . . . and here he comes."

They opened the gate and I got my first look at Ugly, with

Manny bumping around on his back. The bull was bigger than any I'd ever seen. He wasn't as fast as some, but he was strong. Some bulls are turbocharged. This one was like a Hummer. He just kept tossing and taking big long rolls left and right. He pounded all four legs into the ground with a thud, Manny lost his hold, and that was that. "Okay, no score for Manny Rodriguez and another one down for Ugly. Now for some demonstration team roping."

Ugly trotted back toward the pen. I walked around till I could get a better view of him. His shoulder was above my chin. He was brown, with some white dapples on his rump. The wattle under his neck was as wide as my arm, and it swung back and forth making time to his steps. He didn't have a hump like a Brahma but was set more like a short horn in the front, with thick, stubby horns. His ears were fuzzy. Strings of slobber hung from his lips. But his eyes, that was what caught me. They were yellow, not gold or brown, and clean around them was a white ring of eyeball. What gave a bull eyes like that? Was it a natural craziness or was he born mean? He snorted and shook his head like he was thinking of ways to smash cowboys. Watching him pace in the pen, I wasn't thinking he was "Ugly." No, I'd have named him Bull-Dozer. Or better, I'd name this one *Terror-Bull*.

They finished the team roping and let a couple more riders loose on other bulls. Then they moved Ugly up to get the next bull rope on him. He barely fit in the chutes. The cowboy who'd called me a mutton buster was pulling on his glove. I didn't want that guy to win. The music stopped and the announcer said, "Next up is our cowboy come over from

Washoe Valley, right here in Nevada. Ian Marley has made himself pretty well known around the bull-riding circuit, but he's missed out on this bull. Let's see if Ugly's ready for round two."

They opened the gate and it couldn't have gone better—for me. Ugly ran, kicked up with his back legs, then almost sat down. Marley about slid down his back, then Ugly rolled right and did a quick left. It looked like he was fixing to shake that cowboy off. It wasn't two seconds before Marley was brushing the dust from his britches. "Too bad for Ian Marley. Maybe there'll be another go round, 'cause I'm not seeing this bull give up a ride tonight, are you?" the announcer asked the audience. Someone started chanting, "Ugly, Ugly, Ugly." A section of the stands picked it up and cheered for the bull. I felt sweat dripping down my back. Some guys ran out in the arena dressed in humongous cowboy hats that came down past their shoulders and covered up their arms. They weren't wearing shirts and they had faces painted on their bare bellies that they wiggled in time to banjo music. They danced and all the little kids laughed and yelled. I walked toward the chutes. I was next. Darrell was already there.

"Good luck out there, Cam," he said to me.

"You mean it?"

"Sure, as long as you don't take my prize." He grinned.

"I'm hoping on just that," I said.

They had Ugly in a chute for the next go round. The next ground round maybe, and that was me. Captain Hole in the Head. The fairgrounds had a fancy chute for rigging the bulls with the slits up the sides, so we didn't have to fish around for the bull rope. I tossed Ben's bull rope under Ugly to the chute man. He grabbed it and we climbed up our sides of the chute to fix the rope. Ugly snorted and plopped a giant cow pie. "You tried him?" I asked the guy.

"No, you couldn't pay me enough to ride this one."

Great. Well you could pay me. And Ben. Right then I took a breath and shook my head and shoulders. "Okay," I said, and they opened the slide gate and moved Ugly into the bucking chute. I stood over him on the platform and saw the width of his back. It would be hard to grip—my knees were going to sit most straight out. Just then, Ugly reared up and climbed the railings with his front hooves until his head and horns came to my eye level. I jumped back. He swung around like he was going to bash me right there. His head looked as big as a wheelbarrow, and his eye was rolled back and glowing yellow. That look, it was ugly. I swear, he was staring at me. He lunged again, and the platform jerked and rocked from the crash. Three guys took to pushing him back into the chute. They got him calmed down. But me, I could hardly catch my breath.

The announcer started, "Now it's time for another Nevadan. This boy's come all the way from Hawthorne to ride Ugly. He's a newcomer to our bull ring, so let's give it up for Adam Carl." I looked down at Ugly. He was still. I jumped up and down a couple of times. The shaking stopped. My teeth weren't chattering. "Go, Adam!" a kid yelled. I looked in the stands and met his eyes. It was like he looked right into me. I could do it. I felt good. I couldn't help grinning. Cam O'Mara might be a kid who was never sure of a bull, but Adam Carl? He was fearless.

I stepped off the platform and set myself on Ugly's back. Grandpa says you can know something from the feel of a bull, and this one felt thick and stubborn. Cam might have worried, but "Adam" pushed his butt down tighter, laid the bull rope across his palm, and pounded his fingers around it. Then one of us—maybe me or maybe "Adam"—said a prayer, a real one. I mumbled, "Okay, Ben," and then I said, real loud, "Let him go."

✳ **CHAPTER** ✳

TWENTY-NINE

They pulled the gate and this is what I remember. The lights, the dust, and pulling down with my arm and pushing into Ugly with my butt. You can't count seconds when you're riding, but you can feel yourself. I knew I was on, still on, swinging wide, pulling myself hard with my arm, wanting to grab something, anything, lights got brighter, my butt slipped, I struggled for balance.

Then a buzzer. A buzzer. A buzzer. I snapped the bull rope, zipping it through my hand, flew off to my left and hit the ground. It knocked the wind out of me. I came up on my knees and heard a noise like a train coming. It was bull's hooves. I wasn't sure which way to turn. A bullfighter ran past me and another knocked me away and back onto the ground. I looked right up at Ugly's underside as he ran past. I jumped up, scanned for the fence, and ran. It was only when I was safe on the rails that I saw everyone standing and cheering. The announcer said, "And that, ladies and gentlemen, is how you ride a bull. Young Adam Carl from Hawthorne, Nevada, is the winner of the Winnemucca Ugly Challenge. It's a great day for him and a first for Ugly. That's one fine bucking bull, and he moves on to a career in the pro bulls. We can't help wondering if that's where Adam's headed too."

I peered into the crowd. The announcer went on, "There's only one cowboy left in the Ugly Challenge and it goes against the odds, but this next rider could tie with Carl and split the pot. Stranger things have happened, ladies and gents, so stick around, watch our antique wagons and stagecoach circle the field, and after we give that bull some R and R, we'll be back with our last cowboy from right here in Humboldt County, Darrell Wallace."

I don't think anybody else was listening. Everybody was talking and moving around. Mike and Favi ran down the aisle toward me. "You did it!" Favi said. "I knew you could. Well, I hoped you could. . . . Who would believe? . . . oh, it's so good. You did it!"

"Way cool," Mike said. "When did you learn to do that?"

Favi threw her arms around my neck. "Oh, Cam, I was so scared for you."

I hugged her back. Then I turned and wiped my eyes. There was dust in 'em or something. The official guy called to me across the gate. "Come down to the table and we'll get your information for the news story and the check. That fifteen thousand is all yours unless this next guy rides him too."

I told Mike and Favi, "Don't leave without me," and I followed the official past the chutes and out toward the sign-up table. Grandma Jean was already there. Grandpa Roy was behind her. I swallowed hard.

"Good job, son," Grandpa Roy said, shaking my hand. "I couldn't have ridden that bull myself." He grinned and kept pumping my hand. "You ride like a real cowboy. Like an O'Mara, I'd say. Jean, get a picture of us."

"Excuse me," the official said. "First, we'll need you to sign these release forms for the press—they'll want photos and an interview." He handed me a long sheet of heretofores and therefores. A reporter with a fancy camera waved at me and took a step forward, smiling. Right then I knew the Adam Carl thing was going to be a big problem. They couldn't put my picture in the paper with his name.

"I'm not interested," I said.

"We need—" he started to explain to me.

"No, not interested," I interrupted. "Just the check. That's all I want. And make it out to Ben O'Mara."

"It's your money, son," the official said.

"Ben O'Mara is what this young man said, and that's what you'll do," Grandpa Roy said. "It's done, then."

I heard the announcer. "And now for our last bull rider."

"We've got to see Darrell," I said. I ran back toward the arena and watched through the fence. Ugly was in the rigging chute. The announcer went on about Darrell and his wins. Ugly banged the rails and stomped his feet. The announcer kept talking. "Darrell Wallace is one of our homegrown cowboys. He's at home on a bronc or a bull, and he was on the local high school rodeo team. . . ." He kept talking, and talking some more. The men around the chutes were all yelling now. A couple of them sprinted toward the tack room. The announcer was quiet. Some people near him rustled around, whispering. Finally, the mike came back on.

"It seems Darrell Wallace has withdrawn. I'll say it again, ladies and gentlemen, Darrell Wallace has withdrawn from the challenge. That means the Ugly Challenge prize, the full fifteen thousand dollars, goes to Adam Carl, from right here in Nevada. He's the one who rode Ugly."

Darrell was gone? After everything? It didn't make sense.

"Why do you suppose Darrell withdrew at the last minute like that?" Grandpa said. He shook his head. "I don't think I'll ever understand you young people. Well, let's go pick up that check, Cam."

I followed him and Grandma Jean toward the gate. "How'd you know I was here?"

"Favi told me what you were up to last week."

"Man, she promised she wouldn't tell. She shouldn't have told. Not even you."

"She was worried about you," Grandma Jean said.

"And you didn't stop me?" I asked.

"Didn't want to," Grandpa Roy said.

I turned to Grandma Jean. "Is that why . . ."

"I was here to prove who you were. Adam Carl, my grandson."

"Are you mad about me, you know, using him?" I asked her.

"How could I be mad? If he'd grown up, I'd want him to be just like you."

I blushed. We walked by the tack room and I went in to pick up my gear bag. I looked around for Darrell, but his stuff was already gone. Go figure. I'd taken his prize, and he didn't even fight me for it. Manny slapped me on the back, and when I came out to the arena, a bunch of little kids pushed around me asking for my autograph. I took a pencil from one of them and signed a bunch of stuff "Adam Carl." Finally, I met Grandpa and Grandma Jean back at the sign-in table. "Shall we send the check to your Hawthorne address?" the official asked.

"Don't send that money anywhere." I heard a rough voice over my shoulder. I turned and saw the cowboy who called me a mutton buster. "I knew I'd seen this kid. Up in Elko. He's Ben O'Mara's kid brother. I don't know how he got that ride, but I'm telling you, he's not eighteen.

"I'm Adam Carl," I said, quietly.

Red spots popped out on the officials face, and he licked his lips like they wouldn't quite move without the extra spit. "With a challenge to eligibility, I'm afraid we'll have to hold the winnings until we investigate," he said.

Grandpa Roy and I looked at each other. "I rode Ugly. That money's mine," I said. I'd done what no cowboy had done, and now they were keeping my money?

"We can't pay out if you aren't eighteen, son. And since we signed you in without any real ID tonight, if you took the money, that could be fraud. You and your family could be in some real trouble. I'd suggest, if you have any thought that you haven't been honest here, that you let Adam Carl's record stand and forfeit the winnings."

He couldn't mean it. "Can't you just give it to me? I rode the bull!"

"You have to follow the rules," he said. "There might be

other young guys who wanted to try this, but they didn't. They followed the rules. You can't make up your own."

"But it was for Ben," I said.

"Who's Ben?"

"It doesn't matter." I shook my head. "I'll forfeit the prize."

Grandma Jean groaned. Grandpa Roy put both hands on my shoulders as though to hold me steady.

The official scrawled some stuff on a piece of paper saying I'd give up the fifteen thousand dollars I'd just won, and I signed it, "Adam Carl."

✻ CHAPTER ✻

THIRTY

So that's how come, if you look up Ugly, you'll find that Adam Carl won the challenge and it was his first and only bull ride. No one knew what happened to him. Now, I caught up with Darrell Wallace in the parking lot and asked him why he didn't ride. He just said, "You won. I didn't have the heart for it." But I know better. I think he had a heart to do his own thing for Ben, although it turned out neither of us got the money. And as for Ben, well, he was awake when we came home. I went into his room and turned off the TV.

"So, you ready for this?" I said, pulling off my boots and throwing his lucky socks at him.

"For what?" he said.

"I won our bet."

"What bet?"

"You remember. When we had that fight in the barn,

you said if I rode Ugly, then you'd believe anything was possible."

"So?" he asked.

"So I rode Ugly tonight."

"No way."

I pulled the bull rope out of my bag and tossed it on his bed, along with his glove.

"You took my bull rope? Did you think to ask?"

"I didn't want to ask. Get yourself looking decent and come into the living room. We're having company." I went in his dresser and tossed him a clean T-shirt and his comb.

"You gotta *ask* to use my bull rope," he said. "You didn't really ride Ugly."

"Yep, I did. And now company's coming. You look a mess."

"So, who all is gonna be here?" he asked, looking a little more interested.

"Come out and see. It's important—to me."

His eyes lit up, just a little, and he strapped his artificial arm into his walker, grabbed the other side with the good hand, and took a couple of steps to the mirror. He ran the comb through his hair and we walked out together.

Everyone was in the living room. I couldn't look at Mom. Dad was trying to keep from grinning. And Grandma and Grandpa, they were just glowing. Mom had the coffee on, decaf because it was late, and Lali was setting out cookies on the dining room table. Soon enough, we heard trucks in the driveway. The Ruiz family, the Giannis, and Neil and Amy Jones came in.

"So, has Cam told you what he did?" Amy asked.

"Not really," Ben said. "He said he rode Ugly, but he's kidding, right? Nobody's ever stuck on that bull."

"Well, tell him, Cam," she said.

I didn't know how to start. Yeah, I rode Ugly, but I came home empty-handed.

"No need," Grandma Jean said. "I've got it on video." She pulled the tape out of her camera and clicked it into our TV in the living room. I watched Mom. And Ben. There was the flag, and the mutton busters, the team ropers, and the announcer. He was talking about a cowboy from Hawthorne, Adam Carl.

"What?" Mom asked, looking at me.

"Just wait," Grandma Jean said. "It's terrific."

Next, I came out of the chute on Ugly. Watching it was a whole 'nother story than riding it. It wasn't a pretty ride. I was stiff and jerky and Ugly seemed slow. I could see a couple of times, when I was in real trouble—the crowd gasped and I'd leaned way too far to one side or the other, but there I was, up on Ugly, still, and then the buzzer went. I landed, looking dazed, and then the bull turned and came right at me.

"Oh no, Cam." Mom gasped and covered her eyes.

I watched the bullfighters push me down and turn him away and figured I owed them a whole lot—maybe an arm or a leg. Mom peeked at the TV. Anybody could see, they'd saved my butt.

Mom dropped into a chair and looked back and forth from me to Grandpa Roy to Grandma Jean. "You *knew* about this?"

"That's not pertinent," Grandpa Roy said. "Didn't you

see? He rode Ugly. There was a fifteen thousand dollar purse on that bull from the stock company for the first guy to ride him, and it should have been Cam's." Grandpa took a long breath. "But he didn't qualify 'cause of his age. He was doing it for you, Ben."

"You rode Ugly for me?" Ben's mouth dropped open. He gaped at me like that for a second and then he said, "But why?"

"I told you when we made the bet in the barn. If I can ride Ugly, you can do anything. I wanted to get the money too, but . . . I'm sorry, Ben, I wanted money so you could start up your bull-breeding business like you wanted before. . . ."

It was too much. The coolest thing I'd ever done was the most disappointing, too. I didn't want to cry. Not in front of everybody. So I ducked into the kitchen, put my face to the wall, and held my breath, hoping it would stop the tears. Ben's walker clicked on the floor behind me and then I felt his hand on my shoulder. My back heaved and I swallowed the sobs. "I just wanted you back. I thought the bucking bulls you'd always talked about . . ." My words jammed up and wouldn't come out.

Ben put his arm around me, and I leaned into his shoulder and cried.

"It's all right, bro'. It's messed up. This whole deal, it's really messed up. Go on and let it out."

I did. I wrapped my arms around my big brother, buried my head in his shirt, and cried. He squeezed me with his good arm. After a while, I sucked in the snot and wiped my tears on my sleeve.

"I can't believe you rode Ugly. Wow," Ben said. The look

on his face was worth a whole lot. "We'll get along all right without that money, you know."

Neil Jones cleared his throat and stepped into the kitchen. "I don't mean to butt in, but maybe we can help out. Ben, you could come up and work with Amy and learn the ropes in our AI business. It won't be your own, like Cam was hoping for, but we'll pay you commission on your sales, and you can save up and buy some straws of your own to get started. You cross some prize bull's line with some of your crazy O'Mara cows, and it won't be long before you'll have your own breeding business."

I straightened up and looked between them. "Ben, you could pick the stock, Grandpa and I will be the hands, and Mom can do your books," I said.

"O'Mara Bucking Bulls," Ben said with a grin. "Or how about O'Mara *Brothers* Bucking Bulls?"

Lali stuck her head around the corner. "No, it's O'Mara *Family* Bucking Bulls. Don't forget me."

Who could forget Lali?

We had a party after that, and it wasn't just cookies and decaf. It was laughing and joking and Mom getting mad at me for the bull riding. "How could you do that, Cam? You knew I said no."

Grandma Jean spoke right up. "He did it for Ben. You raised a good boy there. He's got a whole lot of 'try' in him, and some good sense too—usually. It's time you trusted him." Then Grandma Jean put her arms around Mom and hugged her until she relaxed.

It was the Giannis toasting Ben, and Favi's dad sitting down with my dad to plot out how to house new bucking stock. It was Ben talking about tomorrow for the first time since they'd put him out of rehab and the Marines. And it was the look on Grandpa Roy's face when he talked about my bull ride. "You should have seen it, Ben. It was like that O'Mara magic just kicked in."

Finally, the company went home, and Dad put Lali to bed. The rest of us sat down at the kitchen table. I looked at Ben. Except for the scar on his skull, he looked the same as he did before he left for Iraq. But I knew how much everything had changed. "I just wish I could fix the rest of it," I said, nodding toward his walker. He teared up the way he does nowadays and punched my shoulder.

"You were stupid to ride that bull. You could have got killed, you know," Ben said. "I still can't figure how you did it. You just started riding. It's not possible."

"It's the salt." Grandpa winked at us.

"Maybe," Grandma Jean said. She went over to the pile of photo albums that Mom kept by the piano and came back with an old one. She thumbed through the fading pages and set it down in front of me and Ben. A young, dark-haired kid stared at the camera from his bike.

I stared back. "That's the kid who yelled at me from the stands tonight."

Ben fixed on the snapshot, then looked around the table, finally resting his eyes on Mom. "I remember now, how it happened. I was in the road after the bomb exploded. I was lying there, playing dead, and this kid came out of nowhere and pulled me off the road. He stayed till my guys came for me." He turned, puzzled, to Grandma Jean. "*That's* the kid."

"Can't be," Mom said. "Don't you remember, Ben? That's your cousin, Adam Carl."

And just then, I believed in all the possibilities. I believed I'd get my brother back one way or another. I believed in Ben's new bull business and in family and the land. And somehow, in that moment, I believed in Grandma's angels.

AUTHOR'S NOTE

✦

Salt Lick, Nevada, is a fictional town, and the characters in *Bull Rider* are fictional as well. But there *have* been a few real bucking bulls called Ugly. I saw Ugly (DK825) walk off a cattle truck and into the Reno Events Center in 2006. He was impressive, and I borrowed his name for the book. There is no "Ugly Challenge," although companies occasionally give cash prizes to cowboys who successfully ride certain bulls on a given night. Like the cowboys from Salt Lick, some bull riders are working cowboys who compete in rodeo on the side, while others are professional rodeo cowboys of the Professional Rodeo Cowboys Association or the Professional Bull Riders. There *is* a Nevada High School Bull Riding Champion—the National High School Rodeo Association sponsors events in forty-five states and provinces in the United States, Canada, and Australia. And there *are* family ranches, like the O'Maras', where people are committed to preserving their traditional way of life—often working both on the ranch and in outside jobs to make ends meet.

Like the fictional O'Maras, thousands of real families have suffered the death or injury of loved ones during the Afghanistan and Iraq Wars, which started in 2001 and 2003. Body armor and improved medical techniques have saved a great number of soldiers and Marines' lives, but many of them come home having lost arms or legs or with traumatic brain injury (TBI). Some suffer from post-traumatic stress disorder or mild forms of brain injury, and you would not know from looking at them that they are victims of the war.

As of early 2008, the Iraq and Afghanistan Veterans of America reported that veterans' advocates believe between 150,000 and 300,000 troops have returned from these wars with some level of traumatic brain injury. They also estimate that one in every three of the approximately 31,000 wounded (through January 2008) have TBI. Some of these men and women will live with the effects of their injuries for years to come. It is up to us to support them, now and in the future.

ACKNOWLEDGMENTS

❊

I depended on many people to inspire and inform me as I wrote *Bull Rider*. I did my best to listen carefully, and I thank them for sharing their stories and their expertise. My deepest thanks to:

Eric Skogsbergh—for a year of e-mails from Iraq

Chris Shivers, Sevi Torturo, and Jake McIntyre, Professional Bull Riders, and Bob Allen and Tuffy, photographers—for interviews and inspiration

Joe Clark, JJJ Bull Riding, Washoe Valley, Nevada—for letting me get up close to the bulls

The Henningsen family—for sharing experiences of ranch life

Todd Gansberg, rancher/bull rider—for ranching expertise

Sandra Musser—for her knowledge of the AI business

Dr. Claire Hall and Rick Riley—for their medical and prosthetic expertise

VA Hospital in Palo Alto, California, especially Patricia Teran-Matthews, Public Affairs Officer; Harriet Straus, Nurse Manager, Polytrauma Unit; and Keleen Preston, TBI Coordinator, Department of Health and Human Services, Office of Disability, Carson City, Nevada—for all their insight on TBI patients

Stanley Williams—for sharing his experiences in the Can Do Unit

Alyen Contreras, Cassie DeSalvo, and Jacob Kavanaugh—for checking skateboarding tricks

Ugly—for inspiring my own Ugly

Emma Dryden—editor and friend

Stephen Barbara—valued agent

Carol Chou—for her editorial insight

Terri Farley and Ellen Hopkins—authors, fellow Nevadans, and friends—and the many friends from SCBWI who supported me through the years

My family.

EDEN WAS ALWAYS GOOD AT BEING GOOD.

Starting high school didn't change who she was. But the night her brother's best friend rapes her, Eden's world capsizes. And she buries the way she used to be.

A *New York Times* Bestseller

★ "This is a poignant book that realistically looks at the lasting effects of trauma on love, relationships, and life. . . . Teens will be reminded of Laurie Halse Anderson's *Speak*. . . . An important addition for every collection."
—*School Library Journal*, starred review

"Don't let a book of this magnitude pass you by. Pick it up and read it because Eden's story demands to be read."
—*Once Upon a Twilight*

★ "AN IMPORTANT ADDITION FOR EVERY COLLECTION."
SCHOOL LIBRARY JOURNAL, STARRED REVIEW

THE WAY I USED TO BE

by AMBER SMITH

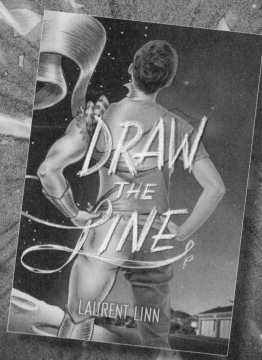

Fig's world lies somewhere between reality and fantasy, where it is hard to tell what is real and what is not. What is fun, and what is frightening. And in this strange world, she must save her mother as her mother slowly descends into madness.

A deeply provocative debut of rare beauty from a new literary voice about the sacrifices a young woman must make to save a person she loves.

PRINT AND EBOOK EDITIONS AVAILABLE
From Margaret K. McElderry Books
TEEN.SimonandSchuster.com

THE POINT OF LIVING IS
LEARNING HOW TO LOVE.

"Brendan Kiely's writing soars off the page, ultimately landing someplace between heartwarming and heart-aching (but definitely somewhere in the heart). Here is a book about music, friendship, first and final loves, and all the blue notes in between. Indeed, *The Last True Love Story* may be exactly that."
—David Arnold, bestselling author of *Mosquitoland*

BEING ADOPTED ISN'T EASY— ESPECIALLY WHEN YOU'RE SEEN AS A NATIONAL ENEMY.

Lily seeks out the roots of her identity in this stirring novel from the acclaimed author of *Crossing the Tracks*.

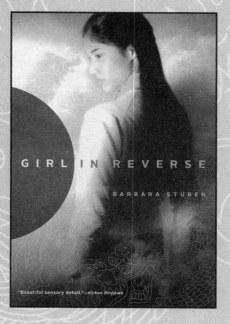

★ "A remarkable journey of self-discovery, inner resilience, and the fragile, surprising, and exquisite complexity of family."
—*Publishers Weekly*, starred review

★ "A diverse cast weaves mystery, romance, and humor into this quest for self-understanding."
—*Library Media Connection*, starred review

"I finished the book in tears of joy and heartache. . . . Stuber deftly overlays a black-and-white canvas with subtle hues to show how the possibility of change can reveal a rainbow of shining truths."
—Elizabeth Wein, author of *Code Name Verity*, a Printz Honor Book